An Emily Lime

mystery

The
BOOK
CaSE

The BOOK CaSE

An Emily Lime mystery

Dave Shelton

David Fickling Books

SCHOLASTIC INC. / NEW YORK

All rights reserved. Published by Scholastic Inc., *Publishers since 1920*, by arrangement with David Fickling Books, Oxford, England. SCHOLASTIC and associated logos are trademarks and/or registered trademarks of Scholastic Inc. DAVID FICKLING BOOKS and associated logos are trademarks and/or registered trademarks of David Fickling Books.

First published in the United Kingdom in 2018 by
David Fickling Books,
31 Beaumont Street,
Oxford OX1 2NP.

davidficklingbooks.com

The publisher does not have any control over and does not assume any responsibility for author or third-party websites or their content.

Library of Congress Cataloging-in-Publication Data available

ISBN 978-1-338-32379-5

10 9 8 7 6 5 4 3 2 1   19 20 21 22 23

Printed in the U.S.A.   23

First edition, June 2019

Book design by Falcon Oast Graphic Art Ltd.

For Ness Wood

ONE

E xcuse me, miss?"

"Yes?"

"Sorry to bother you, but a lady over on the other platform asked me to give you this."

Daphne Blakeway looked round from the timetable she had been examining to find that the man talking to her was a railway porter. He looked old—older, even, than his voice sounded—but harmless enough. He handed her a book. As it happened, Daphne was desperate for something new to read, so she took it from him almost without thinking.

"Oh," she said. "But why? And who?" She scanned the other platform. "The young lady with the dog with the enormous ears?"

"Oh, no, miss. This was an older lady. Shortish, wideish, in a ratty old fur coat. And a hat—so I didn't really get a good look at her ears." The porter squinted across the track. "Can't seem to spot her just at present. Said she was on her way to take the book to St. Rita's herself, but then saw you—she recognized the uniform, you see—and wondered if you might save her the bother. You *are* going to St. Rita's, aren't you, miss?"

"Yes. I was meant to arrive there last night, actually, to start there today, but I got stuck in London when my onward train was canceled."

"Oh yes, that accident outside of Paddington put everything in a right pickle. But would that be all right? The book, I mean. It's for the library, she said."

"Really?" Daphne took a closer look at the book. Her eyes widened as she took in the cover. "*Scarlet Fury: A Smeeton Westerby Mystery*, by J. H.

Buchanan. It doesn't seem quite the usual sort of thing for a school library, I must say."

"Ah well, I suppose you could say that St. Rita's is not quite the usual sort of a school, miss."

"No? Oh, well, in any case, I'll be happy to take the book, of course. Oh, I say, do you know when the next train to Pelham comes in? Only I'm not sure if I've time for a visit to the tearoom."

The porter consulted his pocket watch, holding it at a variety of distances from his bespectacled eyes in an effort to get it in focus.

"Well, miss, let's see . . . Ah yes. Pelham train is due in any minute." He turned to squint away down the track, and indicated a plume of smoke in the middle distance. "See? Here it comes now. But you'll still have time to grab a bun or some such if you look sharp. Old Wilf—he's the conductor—he'll want to fill up his thermos before they set off again. He's a devil if he doesn't have his tea. You get yourself over there and sort yourself a bite to eat—you look like you could do with it. I'll get your suitcase on board, if you like."

"Oh, thank you!" Daphne raised her voice as the noise of the arriving train grew. "That's very kind." She dashed off to the tearoom, stuffing the book into her satchel as she went, leaving the porter to heave her small but weighty case into an empty carriage. When she returned, with some dainty sandwiches in a paper bag, the porter ushered her in through an open carriage door.

"There you go, miss. Your case is up on the rack there. You have a safe journey, now." He shut the door after her.

Daphne poked her head out the open window. "Thank you so much."

"A pleasure, miss," said the porter. "And the best of luck to you at that school of yours." He gave her a little wave, turned, and walked away. "Lord knows you'll need it."

But these last muttered words were lost in the noise of the train getting up steam. The porter raised a smile and tipped his hat to old Wilf the conductor, passing the other way with his freshly refilled thermos. Then, after a suitable pause, he gave a blast on his whistle, waved his flag, and watched as the train pulled away.

Daphne looked out at him from the carriage. She'd had a rotten journey so far, but this funny old man had cheered her with his small kindnesses. She watched him now, half-hidden by steam, patiently helping another passenger—a tall breathless man, who Daphne assumed had just missed catching the same train. Perhaps, she thought, her day had just gotten better, and it would all go smoothly from now on. And as the train picked up speed, she turned her attention to her sandwiches and the book, and she dared to smile a little.

TWO

After the unfortunate incident at her previous school, Daphne's parents had very much welcomed the unexpected letter from St. Rita's offering her a scholarship.

"But it's such a long way!" said Daphne.

"Oh, but it sounds *wonderful*," said her mother.

"And it's free," said her father from behind his newspaper.

"But isn't it all rather odd? How do they even know about me? And why do they want me when I've just been expelled? It all sounds a bit fishy, doesn't it?"

"Now, darling," said her mother, "you know you weren't expelled. It's just that, after the . . ."

"The incident," said her father.

"The incident, yes. Thank you, Rodney. After that, Mrs. Yardley thought your particular—now, how did she put it?—your particular *qualities and enthusiasms* might thrive more fully in an *alternative educational environment.* Perhaps she got in touch with this"—she consulted the letter—"Mrs. Crump herself and recommended you to her."

"I don't think so," said Daphne. She pictured Mrs. Yardley's face the last time they had spoken and concluded that her former headmistress was unlikely to recommend her to anyone for anything. At least not for anything good.

"Well, the letter says that you have 'skills and abilities that would be of great use in our library.' And it sounds like the head—now, what's her name? Oh yes, Mrs. McKay, that's it—she has some very interesting ideas. Very modern. It seems just perfect for you, darling. A nice fresh start."

"And it's free," said Daphne's father.

In the end, Daphne had given in. She was intrigued, and even a little excited and flattered, by being wanted by this odd-sounding school in the middle of nowhere, though she remained, too, suspicious and a little scared. But it wasn't as if she had very much choice in the matter; she had to go somewhere, and at least this way, so far away from her last school, her reputation would not precede her. Perhaps, as her mother said, it could be a fresh start. And they wanted her to help out in the library; that much, at least, Daphne was genuinely excited about. She had never found it easy to get on with other children, but she'd always enjoyed the company of books. And the mysterious Mrs. Crump had been so enthusiastic about her in the letter that Daphne could expect a warm welcome from at least one member of staff. Maybe—just maybe—it would all be all right.

THREE

The journey from Pilkington to Pelham took a little under an hour, along snaking tracks winding through glorious landscape. The countryside, never less than pretty, was made at times breathtakingly beautiful as dramatic shafts of sunlight speared through the gathering clouds, picking out, like spotlights, the crispest details of splendor. It was the pinnacle of nature's art, a real-life masterpiece. But Daphne didn't see a bit of it. She was too engrossed in the book. The awful doings of Mr. Smeeton Westerby, private detective, turned out to be just as despicable and unsuitable as the lurid cover had led her to suspect. The story was violent, ludicrous, sleazy, and entirely unsuitable for children. And Daphne loved every word. She was so thoroughly engrossed in it, in fact, that she didn't notice the conductor entering her carriage at all. He gave a gentle cough. Daphne shrieked and dropped the book.

"Zzorry, miss. I . . . nnn . . . didn't mean to alarm you," the conductor said in a curious, buzzing, nasal voice as Daphne reached down for the fallen book. "But could I see your . . . mmm . . . oh!" His face registered mild surprise as he took in the cover of *Scarlet Fury.* "Ahem. Your ticket . . . nnn . . . please, miss?"

Daphne, blushing, slammed the book shut and placed it facedown on the seat, and then, after much flustered fumbling, produced her ticket.

"Nnnnn . . . vvank you, mmm . . . miss." The conductor examined the ticket, nodded his approval, punched a hole in it, and handed it back. "Pelham . . . mmm . . . izzz the next stop. Will you be needing any help wivvv . . . nnn . . . your luggage?"

"Oh, er, no. Thank you. I shall be perfectly fine. Thank you."

"Very good . . . mmm . . . miss," said the conductor, and with a little bow of the head, he backed out of the door.

As her burning cheeks cooled, Daphne told herself that, actually, she had no need to feel embarrassed about reading such a book as *Scarlet Fury*. It was no work of literary genius, it was true, but the writing had a certain brutal energy that made it more than worthy of her attention. It was really nothing to be ashamed of.

Just the same, she decided to swap its dust jacket with the one from the other book she had with her. Now her copy of *Scarlet Fury* had a lovely picture of a cat on its cover, rather than the gun-toting woman in a flimsy red dress that had so alarmed the conductor.

St. Rita's school was a twenty-minute bus ride from the railway station at Pelham, and quite an unpleasant bus ride at that. The bus was old, dirty, and noisy; the seats were old, dirty, and uncomfortable; and the driver was old, dirty, and terrible at driving. But Daphne ignored it all and carried on reading. The detective, Smeeton Westerby, had just regained consciousness to find himself tied to a chair in a burning building when the bus driver shouted for Daphne's attention.

"Hoy there, love! You wanted the stop for St. Rita's, din't you?"

"Eh? Oh, yes, please."

"Thought so. We're just coming up on

it now. Only, I seen you was deep in that book of yours 'n' likely as not you'd miss it if I din't say nuthin'. Exciting, is it?"

"Oh yes. It's . . . it's *thrilling*!" Daphne gathered up her things and made her way unsteadily toward the front of the bus.

"Is that right?" said the driver. He took a look at the cover. "*Daisy's Little Kitten*, eh? Thrilling, you say?"

"Er, yes."

"Right. Well, to each their own, I suppose." The bus slowed. "Here you are." The driver scanned either side of the road, then opened the door. "Best if I don't actually stop, if you don't mind. It's safer that way, like."

Daphne threw the driver an alarmed look. "Safer for whom?"

"You'll be fine." The driver fixed his eyes on the road ahead. "Just be sure to bend your knees as you land. Quickly now!"

Daphne gulped.

"School's another fifty yards or so, on the right," said the driver as Daphne jumped off. She lost hold of her suitcase as she landed but just managed to stay upright.

"Opposite the bus stop," shouted the driver as the bus sped away.

Puzzled, Daphne watched it go for a moment, then, with a glance at the ominous sky, heaved her suitcase from the ground and set off, trudging toward whatever destiny awaited her around the bend.

FOUR

Actually, it was rather more than fifty yards to the bus stop, a small wooden shelter so densely carved with graffiti that it was a wonder it was still standing. Opposite, set in the high stone wall on the other side of the road, was a tall pair of imposing iron gates. Beside the gates, a carved stone plaque set into the wall read *St. Rita's School for Spirited Girls, Est. 1873.* Beyond the gates, at the end of a long gravel drive, sat the school itself. Even at a distance, it looked dark and imposing, like something from a ghost story. Daphne shivered just to look at it, but she told herself that it was only the foreboding sky that made it look so sinister. Bracing herself, she tried the gates and, finding they were not locked, pushed one open and set off down the drive.

She had not gone far when she saw an odd hunched figure emerge from behind the school and start toward her. As the figure drew closer, Daphne realized that its odd posture was due to the wheelbarrow it was pushing. And as it got closer still, Daphne realized that it was not a gardener, as she had first assumed, but a boy.

"Hullo. Your name Daphne, is it?" The boy parked the barrow in Daphne's path and gave his nose an enthusiastic scratch.

"Yes," said Daphne, putting down her suitcase. She studied the boy for a moment. He was a grubby, scruffy specimen: Everything he wore was crumpled, grimy, and the wrong size for him; he had an odd smell about him, of something faintly exotic but distinctly unpleasant; his hair was enthusiastically berserk. And he wore a school blazer with, to Daphne's surprise, a St. Rita's badge on the breast pocket.

"Grand! You finally made it," he said. "I saw you from inside. Thought you looked like you were struggling with that suitcase a bit."

"I was rather," said Daphne, with a little nod and a smile, and held the case out toward him.

"Thought so," said the boy. "Should be easier with this, though." He tilted his head toward the barrow. "Come on." He turned and started shuffling back toward the school, leaving the wheelbarrow behind him. "I should get a move on, if I were you. Reckon it's going to start tipping down any minute now."

Daphne stared after him in amazement, then glanced

17

up at the sky, which, in turn, glowered back down at her. Sighing, she turned the wheelbarrow round, heaved the suitcase up into it, and set off down the drive. It *was* easier, but it wasn't *easy.* The barrow was difficult to steer and not suited to gravel, but Daphne struggled along, zigzagging down the drive, and soon caught up with the dawdling boy.

"I'm George, by the way," said the boy as Daphne drew up alongside him. "Oh, mind the dip." He pointed to a deep hollow in the driveway just ahead of them. Daphne swerved sharply to avoid it.

"Crikey!" she said when she had wrestled the wheelbarrow back on course. "What happened there?"

"That's what happens when you trust a bunch of third years to fill in a crater."

"A crater? But surely the Germans didn't bomb anywhere near here? And anyway, it's years since the war ended."

"Oh, it were nothing to do with a bomb."

"Oh? What, then?"

"Chemistry experiment. Couple of girls messing about with stolen supplies. Mrs. Klinghoffer was furious."

"I'm not surprised! Were they all right?"

"Dunno. Nobody saw where they landed."

They had arrived at the school itself now, but rather than approaching the front door, George led Daphne round to a path at the side of the building.

"It all looks a bit different in real life," said Daphne, glancing at the shocking state of the brickwork while struggling to keep the barrow from veering into the lavender bushes. "From the drawing in the brochure, I mean."

"Oh, you mean the crumbling walls and the holes in the roof and suchlike? Yes, the old place could use a lot of work, really. But Mrs. McKay, the headmistress, wants the caretaker to do it all because she won't pay up for all the roofers and builders and carpenters and such that it really needs. And he's a nice chap, Mr. Thanet, but really he's a bit useless at anything practical, and really slow. Do you see those broken windows up there? They've been like that for weeks."

"What happened to them?"

"Motorcycle accident."

"On the second floor?"

"Yes. Bloomin' disgrace, it was. Very irresponsible." George shook his head. "Shocking way for a Latin mistress to behave. Here we are." They had reached a door at the rear of the school. George turned the iron handle.

"In the nick of time, too," he said, casting a look at the sullen sky. "It'll be bucketing down soon, I reckon. Ooh, and here comes Mr. Thanet."

Daphne glanced back over her shoulder to see a rather angry-looking bearded man stalking across the playing fields in their direction.

"I don't think he's very happy about you borrowing his wheelbarrow, you know," said George. "We'd probably best make ourselves scarce. Come on."

"Me? But I didn't..."

But George had already gone in, and after one brief glance at Mr. Thanet's face, Daphne heaved her suitcase out of the wheelbarrow and followed.

Inside, hurrying as best she could along the corridor, Daphne noted that the interior of the school had a lot in common with the exterior: It had clearly once been grand and impressive, but was now distinctly worn and neglected. The lower, wood-paneled section of the wall was badly scuffed, while the wallpaper on the upper section was torn and beginning to peel. Pausing for a moment, Daphne poked an exploratory finger under a loose fold of the wallpaper, then squeaked in alarm as half a yard of it rolled itself up from the bottom like a roller blind,

exposing crumbling plaster beneath. A small cloud of fine white dust enveloped her and set her coughing.

"Ooh, don't do that!" George called back to her, casting a worried look at the wall. "It's only the wallpaper holding this place together, I reckon. If you go tearing bits off willy-nilly, then the whole lot might come tumbling down. Might not be such a bad thing, mind, but I'd rather be outside when it happens." He set off again.

Daphne flapped at her uniform to brush off the dust and dashed round the corner after George, straight into the path of a small, red-haired girl coming the other way. Daphne just had time to register the look of surprise on the other girl's face before she slammed into her and down they both fell in a tangle, her suitcase flying off across the floor in one direction, her satchel in another, spilling its contents as it went.

"Oh, I'm so sorry!" said Daphne as she unknotted her limbs and got up.

"Well, I should hope so!" said the girl, already back on her feet, pacing, and looking for something on the floor. "Tearing round the place like that!" Then she snatched up a sheet of writing paper and an envelope. Only then did she look over at Daphne, now busy gathering up her own things, and give her an apologetic smile. "Sorry, that was rude. And . . . and actually it was my fault, too. I wasn't looking where I was going. I had my nose in this letter from my uncle. He's . . . well, he had some . . . rather bad news, I'm afraid, so I was a bit distracted."

She stuffed the letter into her pocket. "Here, let me

give you a hand." One of the books was at the girl's feet. She stooped to pick it up, then glanced at the cover.

"Oh!" The girl stared, shocked, at the book, wrapped in the scandalous cover of *Scarlet Fury*.

"It's . . . it's not mine," said Daphne, plucking it from the girl's hands and stuffing it back into her satchel.

"No, I . . ." The girl seemed stunned, staring into space.

Daphne assumed she must be a sensitive type. The girl blinked, gave her head a little shake, and appeared to recover herself a little. "Don't worry. Your, umm . . . your secret's safe with me."

"Oh, there you are!" George had reappeared. "I was nattering away to you, and I only just realized you weren't there anymore. You missed some good stuff, too. I was being really fascinating. Oh, hello, Veronica." He gave the red-haired girl a nod. She nodded back in a distracted sort of way.

"Got to . . . go," she said, and dashed off.

"Odd girl," said Daphne.

"Yes, well, you'd best get used to those," said George. "This place is full of them. Now come on. It's time you met the boss."

23

FIVE

There was a small set of steps leading up to the library door. George stood at the top with his hand on the door handle, craning his neck to smile back at Daphne.

"I think you're going to like this," he said.

Daphne thought she probably wouldn't. Her expectations had been worn away by everything she had seen so far. Given the state of the rest of the school, it was pretty obvious what to expect: a ratty little room with some ratty old bookshelves full of ratty old books. She forced a smile and prepared to politely smother her disappointment.

George pushed the door open.

"Oh, but do try to keep quiet," he whispered as he stepped inside.

"Of course," said Daphne, following him in, rather annoyed that he'd thought it necessary to say such a thing. She knew how to behave in a library, after all. She was always quiet and respectful. There was no need to tell her.

Then she saw the library and let out a loud gasp.

"Shh!" said George.

"Sorry," whispered Daphne. "It's just that it's so . . ."

It was amazing. It was immense. It was magnificent.

They had entered several feet above floor level, at the top of a short staircase leading down into the vast space of the library, and this elevated view allowed Daphne to get some sense of the size of the place, which, had she been down amongst the maze of bookcases, might have been difficult to grasp. Daphne had never seen so many shelves. It was like a vast and complex world built entirely from bookcases. Good ones, too. Newly made from fine dark wood, with obvious care and skill, to exactly fit the space. Tall arched windows set high in the far wall let in the light of the afternoon sun and cast the whole scene in a magical, golden, honeyed glow.

"Wow!" said Daphne.

"It *is* impressive, isn't it?" said George.

"It's astonishing," said Daphne. "It really is. I never could have imagined." She frowned delicately and paused a moment. "But, um, where are all the *books*?"

It wasn't that there were *no* books in the library. There just weren't very many. What there were would have looked like far too few even at the much smaller library in Daphne's old school. Here, dotted amidst the gaping spaces of the many shelves, they looked pathetic, like the last few teeth in the mouth of an old man who loved sweets but was allergic to toothpaste.

"Eh?" said George, who had padded down the stairs to floor level and seemed to be scanning the room, looking for something.

"I said," said Daphne, "where are all the books?"

"Ah!" said George. "You noticed that? Very good. Impressive librarian instincts, if I may say so. Just what we're after." He smiled at her, looked around him warily, smiled again. "Temporary matter, nothing to worry about. We'll have some new ones soon." He took another couple of steps, still looking around the place as he went. "Still not enough, but, you know, a few more. Oh, and we do have one good section now. Let me show you. I just got them shelved this morning." George tiptoed off behind the bookcase nearest to him, and Daphne followed. Turning the corner, she found herself facing a set of shelves that was stuffed full of books.

"Daphne Blakeway," said George, "let me introduce you to crime!"

"Well, that's a bit more like it!" said Daphne. "Seems an odd choice for a school library, though. Cops and robbers and so forth."

"Oh, well, the girls here like that sort of thing. Well, maybe not the cops so much . . ." George skulked off round another bank of shelving, disappearing from

Daphne's view. "And, you know, it's a start at least, as we try to get things sorted after the ... ah ..."

"After the what?" said Daphne once she had grown tired of waiting for George to continue. Then, when this gained no response, she followed the way George had gone and found him holding a chair out in front of him and trembling. "What *are* you doing?"

"Oh, er ... nothing. Nothing to worry about." George gave Daphne his best effort at a reassuring grin. "Oh, but mind you don't slip on that blood."

He dipped his head to indicate where he meant.

Daphne looked down and saw that just beyond the toes of her shiny new school shoes there was indeed a small puddle of a dark, slightly lumpy liquid. A dotted line of smaller drips of the same color led away past where George was standing.

"Ew! What on earth ... ?"

"Er ... I'll explain later."

There was a sound. Something beyond the next set of shelves. A low rumble and a malignant hiss and some unpleasant crunching, all at once. Daphne shuddered.

"Hang on," said George, and advanced out of view, the chair wobbling in his shaking hands. Then something noisy happened out of Daphne's sight. There was some mildly terrifying animal screeching, some thumps and scratches, some squeals of alarm from George, then a final cry of "Go on! Get off"—a farewell snarl—and a scritchy-scratchy, hurtling scurry of clawed feet racing away across wooden floorboards. Daphne glimpsed a large, dark, furry blur dropping into the bushes outside a high open window.

George reappeared, even more disheveled than he had begun.

"Sorry about that. Now, where was I?" He set down the chair, and because one of its legs seemed to have been torn off, leaving only a splintered stump, it fell over.

George gave it a brief, gentle frown. "Oh yes . . . so, we're trying to get things started again, after the fire."

"What was . . . What fire?"

"The fire that burned down the old library. Terrible, it was. We lost everything. And the bloomin' insurance company refused to pay up for it." George scowled. "They said it'd been started deliberately."

Daphne gasped.

"I know," said George. "It's outrageous. Said they found gas-soaked rags, but if they did they must have put them there themselves. None of our girls would've been so sloppy!"

He led Daphne away from the bloody puddle and back toward the crime section. "But bloomin' Mrs. McKay didn't even put up a fight. So we didn't get a penny, and we'd already spent all the money we did have on swanky new shelving, so now we've nothing left to buy books with. All we've got is a few odds and ends donated by parents. Most of it's rubbish, of course. But these are all right."

He pointed at the neat ranks of crime books.

"Although," George went on, pointing at the one gap on the shelf, "I can't find this one for the life of me. I just hope it turns up before the boss notices or—"

"George, are you doing *any* work today? Oh!"

A small girl in wonky glasses and a beret had emerged, seemingly from nowhere. She looked at George, then at Daphne, then back at George, frowning throughout.

"And who's this?" She pointed a sour expression in Daphne's direction. "And why is she here?"

"This is Daphne Blakeway," said George in an exasperated tone. "We were expecting her, remember? Daphne, this is Emily Lime, assistant librarian."

"Hello," said Daphne. "Pleased to meet you." (Though

31

she wasn't at all sure that she was.) "I was invited by Mrs. Crump, the *head* librarian. Actually, is she here? I ought really to introduce myself and—"

"No," said Emily Lime.

"Oh, but . . ."

"Ah yes," said George. "I should have said. Mrs. Crump is away."

"On sick leave," said Emily Lime.

"For her nerves," said George.

"Indefinitely," said Emily Lime.

"Oh," said Daphne. "Only . . . she's the reason I'm here, really. She approved my scholarship."

She looked from George's face to Emily Lime's, then back again. Her bottom lip fluttered, just a little. "I thought when you said 'meet the boss . . .'"

"Well," said Emily Lime, "in Mrs. Crump's absence, that would be me. And so all new appointments to the library team must be vetted and approved by me."

Daphne bit her lip.

"Oh, don't be ridiculous!" said George. "Just give her the badges, for heaven's sake, and we can all—"

Emily Lime fired a stare at George so hard it might have stopped a charging rhino. "No! I cannot just *give her the badges*. I do not hand out library badges willy-nilly to anyone who asks. There are proper procedures we must adhere to. There is paperwork to fill in. There is a system. There has to be a system!"

She turned her fierce gaze on Daphne. "I'll have to interview her for the position, though heaven knows I have better things to do with my time."

"But I thought—"

Emily Lime raised her hand, like a policeman stopping traffic, and Daphne shut up.

"My office," said Emily Lime. "Ten minutes' time. Don't be late." And with that, she disappeared back the way she had come, grumbling as she went. There was the distant sound of a door opening and then slamming shut.

"Now, don't worry," said George. "You'll be fine."

"Do you think so?"

George rubbed his chin. "Oh yes. You're just lucky you've caught her on a good day."

SIX

Nine and three-quarter minutes later, when Daphne entered the office, Emily Lime didn't even look up from the book she had open on the desk in front of her.

"Hello?" said Daphne. "You said—"

"Shh!" Emily Lime raised a stern finger in Daphne's direction. Daphne shut up.

The pointing finger jabbed downward to indicate a chair on Daphne's side of the desk.

"Oh. Thank—"

"Shh!" said Emily Lime.

Daphne cringed apologetically and pulled out the chair, spilling a pile of books from on top of it onto the floor.

"SHH!" said Emily Lime again, her eyes still fixed on her book, her finger now pointing up at Daphne's face, just in case it wasn't already clear who was making all the noise.

"Oh. Sorry," whispered Daphne as she got down on her hands and knees to tidy up the spilled volumes.

Emily Lime grunted, lowered her finger to the book, and began flipping through the pages at great speed while jotting occasional notes in pencil onto a small card with the other hand. She carried on like this, in silence except for an occasional tut, hum, or grunt, until she turned the final page and closed the book, just as Daphne rose from the floor and took her seat on the chair.

Daphne smiled expectantly across the desk at Emily Lime, who continued to ignore her. Emily Lime opened a small wooden drawer by her side and placed the note-card inside, amongst a stack of others. Then she turned to face forward again, and gave a little start as she noticed Daphne.

"Forgot you were there," she said, with no note of apology in her voice. Then she set aside the previous book and opened up another. She began flipping the pages and note taking once more.

Daphne, seeing that there were three more books after this one in a pile on the desk and that therefore she probably had a while to wait, took the opportunity to look around the room. Books were the main thing about it. There were teetering towers of them on the outskirts of the desktop, piles of them up against the walls, and more on the mantelpiece, on either side of a carriage clock. There were more scattered about the floor and further piles of them balanced on top of various cardboard boxes dotted around the room. Daphne couldn't be absolutely certain, but she felt confident that the boxes were probably full of books, too. Certainly, that would explain why the word *BOOKS* had been written in large black letters on each one.

Daphne turned her face to the window, but swiveled her eyes sideways to watch the girl working away. She was a curious-looking bird, Daphne thought. Her face seemed to be built from twitches. Her lips fluttered, her eyes squinted shut every so often, her stubby little nose danced jerkily, her forehead furrowed and unfurrowed. She looked as if she was reading, though that was surely not possible at the speed she was turning the pages. She was already at the end of another book. She closed its cover, completed her notes, and added the card to the others in the drawer. As she reached for the next book on the pile, her eyes flicked up in Daphne's direction to find her (just in time) staring innocently out the window.

From where Daphne sat, the window gave her a good view of the extensive school playing fields, enclosed on two sides by fences and hedges and on another by woodland. At the edge of the woodland stood a cottage, basking prettily in a narrow band of sunlight that had broken through the gathering clouds. A bicycle leaned against the perfect wooden fence.

A class of girls in PE uniforms ran across the field, away from the school. As the front runners disappeared into the woods, a couple of the slower girls paused by the cottage and entered into what was clearly, even viewed at this distance, a very heated debate. One of the girls strode over to the bicycle and made as if to get on, but the other girl dragged her off it. The vicious fight that followed proved too promising an entertainment for the other runners to ignore, and a mob of them reemerged from the woods to form a ring around the pair, chanting and yelling encouragement.

"Crikey!" muttered Daphne.

Emily Lime looked up at her with a frown, followed her gaze to the spectacle on  the playing field, dismissed it as of no interest, and returned her attention to her book.

Back outside, a man emerged from the front door of

the cottage—she thought it might be Mr. Thanet, the caretaker, but it was hard to be sure at such a distance—and shouted at the fighting girls. This had no effect at all, but then the rain started, hard and heavy, and they hurried off into the woods.

Emily Lime, meanwhile, had returned her attention to her book, but then almost immediately stopped again. She raised her pencil up in front of her face to inspect it, and scowled.

"GEORGE!" shouted Emily Lime, in the direction of the door. "PENCIL!"

The door replied, in a voice very like George's, only more muffled, "What about your bloomin' pencil?"

"It's blunt. I need a sharp one."

"Well, use the bloomin' sharpener, then!" grumbled the door.

"No. Bring me a new one from the box out there."

"I'm busy!" said the door.

"That's right. You're busy bringing me a new pencil. Come on, assistant—assist me!"

"Oh, for goodness' sake!" grumbled the door. "Hang on, then."

The girl tilted her raised finger to point at Daphne.

"Now, what is it you want, exactly?" She held her

pencil out at her side but continued to stare down at the book.

"Er, you told me to come in for an interview. Remember? You said to come to your office in ten minutes' time." Daphne glanced at the clock. "Twenty-six minutes ago."

"Are you sure?"

"Yes."

"An interview? For what?"

"The assistant librarian job," said Daphne.

"*Assistant* assistant librarian," said Emily Lime, finally looking up at Daphne to give her a harsh stare. "Mrs. Crump is the librarian. I am the assistant librarian."

The door muttered a creak as it opened, allowing a very grumpy-looking George to enter. He aimed a friendly smile Daphne's way as he stomped over to the desk, then switched back to glowering as he whipped the used pencil from Emily Lime's outstretched hand and replaced it with a fresh sharp one.

"The vacant post is for an *assistant* assistant librarian," said Emily Lime as George lolloped back out. Emily Lime scrutinized the sentence she had been writing, thought about it for a long moment, and then, with great deliberation, added a period. Satisfied, she laid down the pencil and looked back up at Daphne. "You've read the job description?"

"Job description? Er, no. I haven't *seen* a job description. Mrs. Crump's letter didn't really go into any detail."

"Oh, for heaven's sake!" said Emily Lime. "So unprofessional!" She sighed, drummed her fingers on the desktop, then continued in a weary voice. "Well, it's much as you'd imagine: shelving books, mostly; some filing; after successful completion of your probationary period you get stamping privileges; some dusting and cleaning; and any further duties that may arise, including (but not limited to) organizing reading groups and book clubs, fund-raising, book procurement, catering for senior library staff, accountancy . . ."

Daphne squinted at her.

"Accountancy?"

"Yes. You know: accounts. Money and arithmetic. *Numbers* and so on." She pronounced the word *numbers* with a mixture of bafflement and disgust.

"Well, I . . . I suppose I can give it a try."

Emily Lime frowned and made a note, then briefly considered the tip of her pencil.

"Oh, and pencil sharpening." She made a note to herself on a spare index card. "Any questions?"

"Um, no," said Daphne. "No, that all sounds . . . fine."

"Good." Emily Lime took a form from her desk drawer and laid it on the desktop in front of her. "Right. Standard St. Rita's assistant assistant librarian exam. First letter of the alphabet?"

"Eh?"

"Quite right." Emily Lime ticked a box on the form. "Last one?"

"Oh, zed."

"Just zed, not oh." Emily Lime ticked another box, then scribbled a note next to it. "But I'll accept your second answer. Confident about the ones in between?"

"Er, yes."

Emily Lime ticked the third and final box on the form. "Right. Well, thank you, Miss Bakewell—"

"Blakeway," said Daphne.

"I suppose you'll do. I'm willing to offer you the post on a trial basis. I shall assess your progress halfway through the term and decide then whether to allow you to continue. Your duties begin with immediate effect, starting with—"

"Hang on," said Daphne. "Don't you want to know—?"

"What?" said Emily Lime, sighing aggressively.

"Well, don't you want to know a bit more about me? At least ask me, I don't know . . . what I like to read?"

"Books, I assume. I don't need the tiresome details. Now sign this, will you?" Emily Lime whipped out a sheet of paper from her desk drawer and handed it across to Daphne. "On the dotted line there. Here's a pen."

"What's this for?" said Daphne.

"Standard assistant assistant librarian's contract. Absolutely normal procedure. Just sign it. I haven't got all day."

"But it's blank."

"No, it's not."

"Yes, it is."

"No, it's not. There's a dotted line. See? There."

"Well, yes, I can see there's a dotted line. But there's nothing else."

"Oh, don't worry, I'll put the rest in later."

"That," said Daphne, "doesn't sound right."

"It's fine. Trust me. Or don't trust me and sign it anyway, I don't care. *And* once you've signed, you get a badge. Two, in fact."

Daphne considered this for a moment. She did like badges.

She signed on the dotted line and then, when asked, added her name in capital letters and the date.

Emily Lime snatched away the paper, checked the signature, blew on the drying ink a few times, and put it back in the drawer. Then she got out another sheet and passed that to Daphne.

"This one, too."

Daphne took a look. Again, the sheet was blank except for a dotted line.

"Legal waiver," explained Emily Lime. "In the event that you suffer death, injuries, or other misfortune in the fulfillment of your duties, then the library takes no responsibility. Sign and date. Hurry up."

Daphne signed and dated and handed the sheet back. Emily Lime put it away and then opened up another book.

"George!" she yelled. Then to Daphne she said, "Off you go, then. Don't hang about making the place look untidy."

Daphne stood, glancing as she did so at the tottering piles of books and general dusty clutter about the place.

44

"Well, that would never do," she said as George entered, roughly doubling the total amount of untidiness in the room, and plonked a fresh pile of books onto the desk.

"Oh, there you are," said Emily Lime. She handed him the previous pile. "Here, these are done. Label and shelve, and show"—she paused, concentrated, scowled—"Delia . . ."

"Daphne," said Daphne.

"Daphne—how it's done. Get to it."

"As Your Majesty commands," said George.

Daphne followed him toward the door, but then stopped short and turned back to Emily Lime.

"Oh, but what about my badges?"

"Come back tomorrow." Emily Lime had already opened up another book and was flipping through and taking notes. "Busy now. Go."

And with a gesture reminiscent of someone brushing crumbs from a tabletop, she waved Daphne away.

SEVEN

T here," said George, shutting the door behind them with a practiced kick of his heel. "I told you it'd be fine."

Daphne looked at him in a daze. "But it wasn't fine. It was pretty awful, I think."

"No, it wasn't. It *must* have gone well. You're not even crying."

George led Daphne away from the office door and out of the maze of shelves to an open area filled with tables and chairs.

"I really think she doesn't like me." Daphne shuffled after him.

"Well, no. Of course not." George thumped the books down on a table. "She doesn't like anyone much. Except her blessed books, I suppose. But she'll put up with you better than most, I reckon."

"I'm honored," said Daphne, her voice dripping with sarcasm. "So, what do we need to do with these?" She wafted a hand at the books.

"Oh, well, we use our own system here, but you'll soon get the hang of it. You know the Browne Issue system, I suppose? This is more or less the same but with—"

"Worms!" yelled a voice from the top of the steps. "Library bugs! I need a volunteer—George, that's you! I need you to . . ." The voice trailed off. Its owner, a fearsome blonde girl bracing her arms against the banister at the top of the steps, had the pose of a pirate captain looking

down upon the deck of a ship. She had just spotted Daphne, and her expression suggested that she didn't like what she saw. "Who the *hell* are you?"

Daphne could not believe her ears. There had been some rough types at her old school, but even the worst of them would never say *hell.* She was so shocked that she didn't even consider answering her question. Luckily, George did it for her.

"Cynthia, this is Daphne." George swept an arm emphatically in Daphne's direction. "She's just arrived, and we're all doing our best to make her feel welcome. Well, except Lime, obviously, but we can't expect miracles, can we? Daphne, this is our head girl, Cynthia Rawlinson." He stabbed a dismissive thumb that way. "And I can only apologize."

"Just arrived?" Cynthia fixed her stare on Daphne as she descended the steps, the click-clack of her important-sounding shoes echoing loudly around the library. "But we're not expecting anyone new. I would have been told."

She strode across the floor at a measured pace.

"I don't like surprises."

She leaned in to examine Daphne close up, her head swaying slightly, like a venomous snake hypnotizing its prey before it strikes.

"Who are you, new girl?" She squinted her eyes to dark slits. "Why are you here?"

This seemed to Daphne to be a very good question. At the moment, she felt as if she would much rather be almost anywhere else.

"Daphne's here on a scholarship from the League of Librarians," said George, slightly too loudly, directly into Cynthia's ear. It made her jump and turn her eyes from Daphne's, breaking their spell. "Mrs. Crump organized it all. I s'pose when she left in a hurry some of the paperwork might not have gotten handed on to the head; that's probably why you haven't heard about it. So, what is it we're *volunteering* for?"

Cynthia had looked as if she was going to pursue the matter further, but this change of tack lured her away.

"Oh yes. Mrs. McKay took a telephone call from a Mr. White, who is unexpectedly paying her a visit any moment now. Someone needs to go and open the gates up for his motorcar, and as it's raining that someone is not going to be me. But you bookworms are such drips to begin with that it won't make any difference to you. Once he's inside, take him along to the head's office. And *try* not to bore him to death before he gets there. See to it, Georgie Porgie."

She briefly ruffled his tangled thatch of hair, but then quickly extracted her hand, looked at it, aghast, then wiped it on his blazer, and turned to leave. "Ew, disgusting boy. You need a good soaking. Chop-chop, bookworms. Don't keep Mr. White waiting or there'll be trouble."

The door swung shut behind her.

"Crikey!" said Daphne.

"Yes," said George. "Sorry about that. I was hoping we could steer clear of her for your first day at least. She's a terror, but we're usually safe from her here, thank goodness. I think she must have an allergy to books, which is another good reason to restock the shelves as quickly as we can. Still, we'd better do as we're told, I s'pose. Leave your suitcase—I'll lock the door. Lime won't mind—or notice. She'll be happy in the office for a few hours yet. You've not got an umbrella, have you?"

"I'm afraid not."

"Oh, well, never mind. Maybe it'll have eased off a bit by now."

It turned out that Mr. White's arrival was not quite so imminent as Cynthia Rawlinson had made out. Just half of the long walk along the drive was enough for Daphne to get soaked; by the time they reached the gates and wrestled them open, she was as wet as she thought it was possible to be.

They crossed the road and stood on the verge, sodden, waiting.

"Well," said George, raising his voice to be heard above the thundering rain, "this *is* nice!"

Daphne, though properly miserable, smiled anyway.

"Oh, George?"

"Yes?"

"What was your lion-taming act in the library all about?"

"Eh?" George tried to look puzzled.

"Oh, come on! Something ate half of that chair you were waving about. What was it?"

"Oh, that," said George, as if the whole matter had slipped his mind quite naturally. "That was just the Beast."

"The . . . *Beast*?" said Daphne, shivering a little.

"Yes, the school cat. At least, it lives here. It doesn't actually belong to the school, I don't think." George considered this point for a moment. "More like the other way round, if anything. It can be a bit tricky with . . . well, with anybody, really. But especially new folk. So I turfed it out to be on the safe side. It spends a lot of its time in the library, but mostly sleeping. Mostly it's just a problem when it brings us gifts."

"Gifts? What kind of . . . ?"

"Oh, you know. Dead things. Mice, birds, the usual stuff."

"Ew, that's . . ."

"Oh, and a deer. But that was a one-off."

". . . horrib—did you say *deer*?" Daphne gaped.

"Just a small one. But that was before my time here so, you know, you might want to take it with a pinch of salt."

"Right."

"Anyway, it's not much bother so long as you leave it alone, and you don't make too much noise. It's a proper library cat like that—bloomin' fearsome if you don't keep quiet."

"I see."

"Come to think of it, I wonder if it's related to Emily Lime."

George peered through the heavy curtain of rain down the road. "Oh, is this our man, do you think?"

A dim shadow was growing in the wet haze of the road, and the low rumble of an engine fought its way through the noise of the downpour.

"I jolly well hope so," said Daphne.

George flapped his arms about to flag down the motorcar, and it stopped beside him. The driver leaned across to wind down the window on the passenger side, and George leaned in to speak.

"You Mr. White? Here to see Mrs. McKay?"

He was a neat and tidy-looking fellow in a smart gray suit, with a crisply pressed shirt and a precisely engineered knot in his tie. His hair was slicked back with hair oil. Even in the tiny glimpse that Daphne caught of him, he radiated calm, authority, and control.

"That's right, old man. Through here, is it?" He waved a hand clad in a leather driving glove at the gateway.

"Yes," said George. "Thought we'd better see you in and—"

"Thanks, old sport." Mr. White set the car turning through the open gates.

"Oh, but—"

"Well!" said Daphne. "He might at least have offered us a lift back to the school."

"Probably worried about us dripping on his upholstery," said George. "But he'd be better off worrying about that hole."

The rain, running like a stream down the gently inclining ground, had filled the hole in the driveway, and it now resembled nothing more than a large puddle.

"Oh dear," said Daphne as George flapped his arms in warning.

There was a splash and a crunching noise, and

then there was some shouting. Luckily the noise of the rain kept the worst of Mr. White's curses from reaching Daphne's delicate ears, though she guessed that *hell* would be the least of it.

"Oh dear," said George.

By the time they reached the car—stationary, one wheel underwater and listing alarmingly to one side—Mr. White had abandoned his attempts to restart the engine, climbed out of the driver's side door, and was now ankle deep in the water, staring at the crippled vehicle incredulously. He cried out and kicked one of the tires.

"What in God's name . . . ?"

George leaned over to appraise the situation, then shook his head.

"Oof!" he said. "That doesn't look too clever. Come on, mister—let's get you in out of the wet. I'll see if I can get the hockey team to shift this back onto shore while you're seeing Mrs. McKay."

"But how—?" began Mr. White as George gently led him away toward the school.

"Chemistry experiment," said Daphne. "Don't ask."

*

"So, what is it you're here to see Mrs. McKay about, if you don't mind me asking?" said George as they squelched along the corridor. "Have you got a daughter here?"

"Actually, no," said Mr. White rather abruptly. He was a tall man, but in his current saturated state he walked along bent over as if still hunching beneath the pouring rain. He ran a hand over his head, pushing a mass of hair back off his face. "I do have a niece here, as it happens, but this is a . . . business matter.

Confidential. And very boring, I'm afraid." He managed a perfunctory smile.

"Oh, all right. Mind you, I reckon there's not much that's really boring. Almost anything is interesting if you find the right way to look at it. It's just that some things take a bit more effort, that's all."

"I'm sure you're right," said Mr. White, sounding distracted and swinging his head from side to side to examine each of the doors they passed. He frowned a little more with each one.

"The numbering of your classrooms," he said, "is very . . . odd."

Daphne had noticed this, too. There seemed to be no system to the numbering at all. Room 11 was next to room 47 and opposite room 9B. It all seemed a bit . . .

"Mad, isn't it?" said George. "It was some idea the head before last had. Something to do with *improving memory skills* and *defying expectation* and *thinking in original ways*. Potty, I call it, but you kind of get used to it after a while. Here we are."

Head girl Cynthia Rawlinson was prowling around outside a door a little farther along the corridor. Spotting the approaching group, she loped toward them, smirking.

"Oh dear, is it still raining? How unfortunate. You poor things." Then she noticed that Mr. White was very nearly as bedraggled as the children and her expression changed to one of anger. "Oh, for heaven's sake, you buffoons! Can't you even get a guest safely from their motorcar to the door without half drowning them?"

"Sorry," said George, grinning widely.

Cynthia knocked at the head's door.

"Enter," said a tremulous voice from within.

Daphne caught a glimpse, between Cynthia and Mr. White, of a tall, thin, gray-haired woman rising from behind a desk to greet them.

"Ah! Good afternoon, Mr. White," she said, extending a frail hand. "So good of you to drop by. Oh my goodness, you're wet through. Do take a seat by the fire."

She waved her visitor toward a chair close to an open fire that bathed the room in a warm orange glow.

"Cynthia, my dear," she said, in a singsong voice that in no way matched the scowl that she aimed at the head girl, "perhaps you might fetch us a tray of tea. And a towel. Thank you so much."

Then, glancing up at the door, she caught sight of Daphne, and a look of puzzlement came over her. Daphne gave an awkward sort of half wave before George yanked her away and knocked at the next door along.

"Now then," he said. "I should introduce you to the deputy head, while we're in the vicinity like. I told her I'd bring you along round about now. She's not a bad old stick, Miss Bagley."

"High praise indeed." The formidable-looking woman who had appeared in the doorway gave George an amused grin.

"Oh, hello, mmm . . . miss," said George. "This is Daphne."

"Yes." Miss Bagley turned to Daphne and gave her a warm smile. "Hello, petal. Lovely to meet you. Rather later and wetter than expected, but thank you, George, for managing not to actually drown the poor girl. Now, off you go, you clot. Go and get dry."

"Yes, mmm . . . miss." George lolloped off, trailing wet footprints down the corridor.

Miss Bagley watched him go, smiling.

"That boy!" she said. She shook her head, then turned her attention back to Daphne. "Now, flower, how about a nice cup of tea?"

EIGHT

O h," said Daphne, glancing around the room, "this
is . . . cozy."

"Well, that's one word for it, I suppose," said Miss
Bagley, negotiating her way between a filing cabinet
and a tall tower of books and papers. "It's the *wrong*
word for it, but it's certainly *a* word. A better one might
be *tiny*. Better yet, you could say *broom cupboard*, but
that's two words."

She excavated a plain wooden chair from beneath
more papers and placed it on a small patch of uncov-
ered floor near Daphne.

"Now then, flower, you have a seat. And there's an electric heater somewhere there. If you can find it, then feel free to turn it on and get yourself warmed up."

The delicious tea that Miss Bagley provided came from a huge thermos that she took down from a shelf, and that she poured into mugs from the middle drawer of the filing cabinet. ("*M* for mugs," she said.) The very excellent fruitcake came from the top drawer. ("*C* for cake.") Once food and drink had been suitably supplied, Miss Bagley seated herself on a second chair, facing Daphne at close quarters, their knees almost touching. Daphne's clothes gently steamed in the heat from the electric fire.

"Well, lass, as you can see, the role of deputy head is a position of considerable distinction, as is properly reflected in the magnificence of my office." She indicated their surroundings with a necessarily small wave of her hand.

Daphne giggled.

Miss Bagley smiled back. "Well, first things first: Welcome to St. Rita's."

"Thank you. I'm very pleased to be here," said Daphne, because she was more polite than she was honest.

Miss Bagley looked at her thoughtfully.

"I very much doubt that," she said.

Daphne looked shocked. "No, really—"

"It's all right," said Miss Bagley. "There are some girls who really *are* pleased to be here, it's true, but for all the wrong reasons. Well, for instance . . . have you met our head girl?"

"Cynthia? Yes, I'm afraid . . . that is, yes. Yes, I have."

"Yes. Cynthia Rawlinson. Also known as *the Roar*— but you didn't hear that from me, mind. I wouldn't approve of giving our esteemed head girl a derogatory nickname, however clever."

Miss Bagley took a sip of tea.

"Nasty piece of work, that one. But even Cynthia's

not beyond hope, I like to think. Anyway, as I say, you're very welcome at St. Rita's. You may not—*should* not—be glad to be here, but I'm very pleased that you are."

"Thank you," Daphne said. "But, um, why shouldn't I want to be here?"

"Oh, m'dear, you'd need to be bonkers in the noodle to *want* to be here. It's a dreadful place! But trust me, I think it is exactly where you *need* to be. And more than that, this place needs *you*. It is a terrible school, Daphne, but I promise you this: You may not be taught anything very much by the teachers here—they're mostly hopeless, to be honest—but by heck you will learn some things. And it won't be a terrible school forever. I'm determined it won't be. It's already improved today with you arriving, after all. And it's going to carry on getting better, if I have anything to do with it.

"Now, have you met any of the other girls yet? They're a rum crowd, I'll grant you: rough round the edges, most of 'em—and one or two are rough in the middle, too—but there's plenty who could be proper wonderful given half a chance."

"I met a couple," said Daphne. "Well, two girls and George."

"Hmm, yes . . . George. I'm hoping he might turn out

rather well, eventually. Oh, but don't tell him I said that. I expect you must be wondering what a boy is doing in a school for girls?"

"I am a bit, yes."

"Yes. You would have disappointed me if you hadn't." Miss Bagley paused, but only for the shortest moment. "And you'll have met Emily Lime, I suppose?"

"Yes."

"Yes. Tricky character, isn't she? Bit of an acquired taste, that one. But rather brilliant, in her way." Miss Bagley took a thoughtful sip of tea. "Utterly useless in most other ways, mind. But brilliant in hers. And who's the other girl?"

"Um, I ran into . . . Veronica?"

"Ah. Yes," Miss Bagley said. "Veronica Keogh."

Miss Bagley looked thoughtful as she considered what else to say on the subject, then decided to finish off her cake instead.

"The thing about a place like St. Rita's, Daphne, is you sort of have to find your own way through it."

Miss Bagley set her plate aside and fixed her eyes on Daphne's.

"But I'm confident you will. Give yourself a little while to settle in and you'll be fine. And I'm sure the library, and the school, will benefit from your presence."

She smiled such a warm smile that Daphne really believed her.

"Now, here's your timetable. I've marked the good lessons with stars, the bad 'uns with crosses."

Daphne noted that the stars were very much outnumbered.

"You make your own mind up which ones you turn up to. Library staff have special privileges that way. It's a little quirk of the school rules that they introduced . . . shortly after young Miss Lime arrived, as it happens."

"So, I can choose which lessons I go to?"

"Yes, flower, so long as you still get yourself a good education, you can miss them all if you like. Though you'd be a fool to skip Latin: Miss Cosgrove is inspirational. Terrible motorcyclist, but an excellent teacher. But you make your own mind up. There'll be exams to take at the end of the year and you'll need to pass them, but how you learn is up to you. I'd suggest, personally, that you do a lot of reading. Once the library's got some decent books in, that is. Now then, you'd best take a look at your dorm and get settled in. I've asked one of the girls to—"

There was a knock at the door.

"—take you up and show you around. Come in, Marion."

The door opened and revealed a stout girl of roughly Daphne's own age, beaming at her with a hearty smile. In one hand she was holding Daphne's suitcase as if it weighed virtually nothing. The other hand she thrust toward Daphne.

"Marion Fink. Welcoming committee," she said. "Pleased to meet you, new bug. Come along, old thing, and I'll show you to your quarters."

"Off you go, then," said Miss Bagley.

"Thank you," said Daphne, rising from her chair and picking her way to the door.

Miss Bagley saw them out and watched as they walked away off down the corridor.

"And good luck," she said.

NINE

M arion was barreling along the corridor toward the stairs at such a speed that Daphne almost had to run to keep up.

"Dorms are two flights up. Hope you're fit for a climb," said Marion. "Can't give you the full tour, I'm afraid. I have to meet my chum Cicely. Help her out with her biology. But I'll get you settled in."

"That's . . . very kind . . . of you," gasped Daphne, already a little breathless.

"Jolly dee. Well, I suppose you'll want to unpack first. Hope you don't mind—bumped into old George, and he

mentioned you'd left
your suitcase in the
library so I took the
liberty of fetching it
along. This
all you've
got?"

"Oh. There
was . . . another . . . case.
That was . . . sent on ahead. It should . . . have arrived . . .
yesterday."

"Oh yes. Think I saw it up there. Old Thanet brought
it up. Nearly blew a gasket getting it up the stairs! Good
lock on it, is there?"

"I, er . . . I don't know. I . . . suppose so. Why?"

"Oh, no reason, old thing. Just taking an interest, you
know."

"In a . . . lock?"

"Well, you see there's plenty of gals in this place who
take quite an interest in locks. Just hope nobody's taken
too much interest in yours."

"Oh . . . heavens!"

"Not to worry, old thing. It's not as if any of the girls
are likely to have stolen anything."

"Thank goodness! I—"

"No. Most likely they'd just hold anything decent to ransom. Probably do you a discount, too, as a new girl."

"What?"

"Oh yes. They can be jolly decent like that."

They reached the top of the first flight of stairs, giving Daphne a brief moment of respite from their exhausting ascent. Then Marion set off up the second flight with renewed vigor. Daphne scurried along in her wake.

"So, I hear you've been brought in as a bit of a library whiz, eh? Bit of a book fan? Can't say I've bothered much with the library myself. Never quite hit it off with Old Crumpy. I folded over some corners to keep my place once; turned out that particular book was something important—illuminated by monks or some such—and Crump had a fit. Couldn't see what the fuss was about personally. Not as if it was new, after all."

"What . . ." wheezed Daphne. "What was it that . . . happened to Mrs. Crump, exactly?"

"Oh, well, funny old business. She'd been working in the library one evening and nodded off. Next thing she's screaming the place down saying some fella had broken in. Burglar or what have you."

"Heavens!"

"But all the doors were locked and there was no sign of a break-in, so the old girl must have just dreamed it. But there was no telling her, and she was such a bag of nerves afterward that she was no earthly use, so the head chucked her out on sick leave and no one's seen her since."

They arrived at last at the top of the staircase.

"Crikey!" gasped Daphne, as much in response to the speed at which her heart was beating as to the news of Mrs. Crump's departure.

Now that they were no longer climbing stairs, Marion was able to demonstrate her superior turn of speed on the flat, and sped off, Daphne's suitcase swinging at the end of her arm like the pendulum of an overwound clock. Daphne wearily set off in her wake. Luckily, they hadn't far to go.

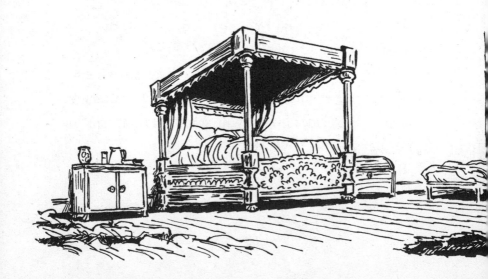

At a ratty door, Marion came to an abrupt halt, gave the doorknob a firm handshake, and barged in. Daphne stumbled in after her.

The dorm, besides its general messiness, was more or less as Daphne had expected, except for two things.

The first thing was the enormous four-poster bed at the far end of the room. All the other beds were simple, metal-framed singles, almost all with their sheets and blankets messily hanging off them. The four-poster was grand and imposing, made of a dark-stained wood, ornately carved, and with plush drapes hanging from its upper section.

"Whose is that?" said Daphne, goggle-eyed.

"Oh, that one's mine," said Marion. "Bit embarrassing, really, but Daddy went to so much trouble sending it here I didn't feel I could refuse it."

"Your bed has a roof!"

Marion laughed. "Well, yes, I suppose so."

The second thing was that there was a hole in the floor.

"And, um . . . why is there a hole in the floor?" said Daphne.

Marion, despite having just leapt nonchalantly over it, seemed for a moment not to have a clue what Daphne was talking about.

"Eh?" she said, turning back to face her. Then, following the line of Daphne's gaze, her own eyes fell upon the hole and understanding took hold. "Oh, *that*? Don't worry about *that*. You'll soon get used to it. You'll quite forget it's there."

"I hope I shan't," said Daphne, edging warily around the ragged gap in the floorboards at as much of a distance as the beds allowed. "What happened?"

"Oh, usual sort of story. Fanshawe had stolen my cannonball, hid it on top of that wardrobe over there. Then a couple of the other girls got into a bit of a tussle and, hey ho, bashed into the wardrobe and toppled it over. High center of gravity, what with the cannonball being up there and all. You know, physics and all that bosh. Wardrobe falls over, cannonball hits the floor and goes straight through into the room below. Lucky it wasn't during lessons or someone would have copped for the most frightful headache! Probably woodworm, I reckon."

"Your *cannonball*?"

"Eh?"

"You have a cannonball?"

"Yes, well, *had* a cannonball, anyway. Course the Roar confiscated it after that little to-do."

"Why did you have a cannonball?"

"Oh, I borrowed it from home and brought it in to show Mrs. Quigley—she's the history bird here. Thought she'd be interested. It's pretty old, I think."

"Borrowed it?" said Daphne. "From home?"

Marion looked at her as if she were dim. "Yes. It's all right. Daddy's got dozens of them at the castle. It's not as if he'll miss it."

"Your father lives in a castle?"

"Yes. Oh, but it's only a small one."

"Oh. Of course."

"Can't afford to heat the big ones, you see, so he only uses those in the summer. Anyway, enough chitchatting. I must push off. This is your bunk."

Marion indicated the one bed with neatly made-up covers on it.

"Looks like your luggage has survived."

She prodded a finger at the large battered case on the bed while parking Daphne's other case on the floor beside it.

"Yes, I suppose I ought to unpack," said Daphne, stooping to examine some fresh scratch marks around the keyhole of the lock. "If someone else hasn't done it for me already."

Marion leaned in for a furrowed glimpse.

"I see what you mean. Looks as if someone's been trying to get in. But did they succeed? That's the question."

"Oh, the beasts!" said Daphne. "Well, they'd better not have filched my books or I shall . . . I shall . . . well, I don't quite know what I shall do, but they had better watch out, that's all!"

"Think you'll be all right, Daffers. Looks like pretty amateur work to me. Probably Peasgood or Walton—neither of them much cop at lock picking, and not what you'd call big readers either. Now Peters, in the lower sixth year, is another matter, but she wouldn't leave a mark on it. Absolute whiz with a hairpin, that girl. But these fourth-year squirts are very hit-and-miss."

Daphne had fished out the key from her pinafore pocket and fumbled it into the keyhole. But it wouldn't turn. She grunted in frustration and gave it a violent wiggle, but it wouldn't budge. She tried brute force with no better result.

"Oh, blast it!" she cried, and gave the lid a well-deserved whack with her free hand to punish it for its lack of cooperation.

Instantly the case burst open. The lid sprang up, and clothing spewed out of the case's gaping maw, shooting toward Daphne's face. Shocked, she leapt backward, lost her balance, and toppled into a heap on the floor (thankfully a safe distance from the hole). She was quickly covered by a torrent of clothing.

"Well, that's got it open anyway," said Marion, unhelpfully. "Think you may have had it a bit overstuffed, if you don't mind me saying. Positively spring-loaded. Like a jolly old jack-in-the-box."

Daphne clawed a white cotton blouse off her face to allow her

to glare up at Marion. It was a pretty hefty kind of glare that might easily have felled a weedier girl at twenty paces, but Marion was oblivious.

"Crikey, if you could have seen your face. You were quite a sight, I must say."

"So glad I could offer some entertainment," said Daphne, rising to her feet and brushing a gym sock from her hair.

Marion caught her icy tone. "Sorry, old thing. Here, let me help you tidy up."

She bent to scoop up a nightdress, a hot water bottle, and a pencil case while Daphne began to gather together her underwear.

"Does it look like everything's still here?"

"So far as I can tell," said Daphne. "I think so . . ."

She dumped a hillock of knickers and bras on the bed and then draped a blouse over the top for modesty's sake. Then she took stock of everything still in the case and the items Marion was holding, and then scanned everything that remained scattered over the floor, ticking off items on the list in her head as she did so.

"Oh, but where's Edgar?"

"Teddy bear?" said Marion.

"Yes," said Daphne, blushing a little. "Well, a rabbit. And, er, more of a lucky mascot, really."

"Of course, old thing. Don't think I see . . ." Marion set down her own armful of things on Daphne's bed and passed her steely stare over the floor, then pointed. "Oh, is that it, under there?"

Daphne knelt down and reached under the next bed along, passing her hand in a sweeping motion over the floorboards.

"Crikey, it could do with a clean under here! Oh, is that . . . ?"

She pulled out her arm. In her hand was a stuffed toy.

"Oh, bad luck. Kangaroo. Wrong sort of hopper, eh?" said Marion.

"Yes, I—"

"Oh, wait. Is this the fella?" Marion held aloft a pale blue, well-worn toy rabbit.

"Oh. Yes!"

"Landed in the wastepaper basket. Heck of a shot! You a netball whiz or something?" said Marion. She brushed the worst of the dust off the rabbit and handed him back to Daphne.

Daphne clutched him briefly to her chest, then remembered herself and affected a more nonchalant air.

"Thanks," she said. "Silly old thing, really. Don't know why I hang on to him, in fact."

"Of course, old girl," said Marion, watching with a smile as Daphne placed Edgar, with tender care, onto her pillow. "Right, I need to push off and . . . Oh, hello there."

Opening the door, Marion had revealed the small red-haired girl, Veronica, and another girl twice her size about to come in. They both looked surprised to find the dorm occupied.

Veronica and the big girl parted to allow Marion out, then the big girl exchanged a quiet word with Veronica and disappeared from view. Veronica stepped smiling into the dorm.

"Hello again. How funny to—oh!"

Veronica's face fell. She stared at Daphne with fierce concentration and strode quickly over to her, her hand pushed out ahead of her as if she meant to push Daphne over. Daphne froze, braced herself for the blow, but instead Veronica snatched the kangaroo from Daphne's hand and held it close to her chest.

"Please . . ." she said in a shrill voice, then looked down at the toy in her hands and took a breath.

"Please," she said, her voice normal now, "don't touch RooRoo. She was a present from my mummy and . . . oh, I know it's silly . . . but I just don't like anyone else touching her."

"Sorry," said Daphne. "I didn't . . ."

"No. Of course, you couldn't know."

Veronica laid the kangaroo on the bed next to Daphne's and then straightened the bedclothes just enough to tuck her in. Then she turned back to Daphne and smiled again.

"So, it looks like we're neighbors."

"Er, yes."

"I'm so glad," said Veronica. "I think I must have made a bad first impression on you—and a bad second impression in fact—but I'm sure we shall be friends." She pointed at Daphne's cases and satchel. "Can I help you unpack, to make amends?"

"Well, that's very kind of you, but actually, I was going to leave that for now and get stuck into some"—Daphne consulted her timetable—"chemistry, with Mrs. Klinghoffer, in room 93."

"Chemistry?" said Veronica. "You're brave."

She looked Daphne up and down, seeming to consider something. Then she jumped off the bed and skipped toward the door.

"Come on, then. I'll show you the way."

Veronica chattered away happily to Daphne as she led her down the stairs and along a seemingly endless succession of winding corridors to room 93. Daphne thought how sweet it was of her to make so much effort to be friendly. But then, as soon as they arrived at the chemistry laboratory, Veronica deserted Daphne with barely a word to join the big girl, who had saved her a place at the front of the class. It seemed to be the last seat there was, as the room was packed full of eager girls, filling the air with an expectant buzz of excitement. Daphne was still looking for somewhere to sit when George and Emily Lime, her nose in a book, appeared at her side.

"Standing room only, I see," said George. "Come on."

He led them to a spot at the back of the room where, positioned behind some of the shorter girls, they at least had a partial view.

"How come chemistry is so popular?" said Daphne.

"Because of Mrs. Klinghoffer," said George.

"Oh, is she good, then?"

A derisory snort emerged from behind Emily Lime's book.

"No. She's just blind as a bat. But even then, she doesn't normally get this kind of a turnout." George gave his chin a thoughtful scratch. "I reckon something's up."

"What do you—?"

"Quiet!"

Daphne peered over the frizzy curls of the girl seated in front of her to take in her first sighting of Mrs. Klinghoffer, tall and sturdy, staring through impossibly thick spectacle lenses over the heads of the class.

"Please be being quiet now, yes? You know what I am always saying, class?"

"SILENCE FOR THE SCIENCE!" chanted the girls in reply.

"Ha! Yes. This is right. You are good girls, yes?" Mrs. Klinghoffer squinted into the mass of girls. "And there are so many of you here, I am thinking."

She leaned in until her nose was almost touching the face of a girl in the front row.

"Ah yes! There is one of you now! How marvelous! Now today, oh, we are having such an exciting lesson! But you must all be helping me and being very good and clever and sensible, yes?"

"YES, MISS!" chanted the girls, though Daphne thought she heard a less optimistic grunt from Emily Lime.

"Excellent!" Mrs. Klinghoffer clapped her hands in delight. "Then let us be making the science, yes?"

TEN

M rs. Klinghoffer! Mrs. Klinghoffer! Are you there? Are you all right?"

Daphne stumbled through thick smoke, her arms outstretched.

"I'll open a window," said George from somewhere nearby. "If I can find one."

"Good idea."

Broken glass crunched beneath Daphne's foot on the wet floor.

"Mrs. Klinghoffer!"

Around her was unseen chaos as girls shrieked and ran about. One of them briefly emerged from the haze, collided with Daphne, then bounced off, giggling, back into the smoke.

"Is chemistry always like this?"

"Well," yelled George, some distance off now, "the explosions aren't usually quite so big, but yes, more or less. Ah, here we—ow! Dalby, was that you? Mind your bloomin' elbows, can't you?—I found the window."

"Jolly good. Now if I can just find—ah!"

Daphne stopped in her tracks as the tall figure of the chemistry mistress emerged from the murk. Daphne was relieved to see her still standing, after the recent drama of the preceding lesson. Then, on closer inspection, that relief was quickly replaced by fresh alarm.

"Mrs. Klinghoffer!"

"Yes, yes, child. Do not be worrying. Everything is being quite all right and I am being fine." Mrs. Klinghoffer raised her voice. "But if anyone is finding the fire extinguisher, then can they please be bringing it to me so that I can be putting out my hair. Thank you."

Later, though the rest of the class had fled, Daphne, George, and Emily Lime stayed behind and helped

Mrs. Klinghoffer clear up the mess. Or rather, Daphne made Mrs. Klinghoffer sit down out of the way while she and George cleared up. Emily Lime just sat at a desk reading.

"That was quick work from that girl with the fire extinguisher," said Daphne, mopping the floor. "And it can't have been easy aiming it, with all the smoke making it so hard to see."

"No. Although Mrs. K was kind of like a beacon once the fire really took hold."

George tipped a dustpan's worth of broken glass into the bin.

"Yes. Do you think the girl with the extinguisher knew it was a wig before she squirted it off?"

"I'm sure. The legend of Mrs. Klinghoffer's hair is pretty well-known."

"Did she lose her real hair—?"

"In a previous lesson? Yes. Well, first some second years turned it purple. This was a year or so ago. Then a few days later, the fifth years said they'd worked out how to fix it. Coated it in heaven knows what, and it all fell out. Although to be fair, it did more or less turn back to its original color first. And they did stump up for the wig."

They glanced over at Mrs. Klinghoffer, now reunited with the wig, though for all their efforts to arrange it, it sat on her head like a half-drowned guinea pig.

"We'll leave the window open, miss, to let the rest of the smoke out," said Daphne.

"Oh, is there being smoke?" said Mrs. Klinghoffer, gazing about her, then squinting at close range at George for a moment. "Well, thank you, girls."

"You're welcome," said George, in the deepest voice he could manage.

Mrs. Klinghoffer turned to address the empty lab. "Very well, then, class. I hope you were all finding that informative. Please be writing up the experiment in your best handwriting in your exercise books before our next lesson, yes? And not quite so much tomfoolery next time."

George and Daphne exchanged shrugs and made for the door, closely followed by the book-faced Emily Lime.

"Class dismissed," said Mrs. Klinghoffer to the empty room. "And no pushing on your way out!"

ELEVEN

Y ou survived, then?"

Daphne looked up from her book and over at
Veronica lying in the bed next to hers.

"Eh?"

The two of them were amongst a select few of the
fourth-year girls who were actually in their beds. Most
of the others were still up, and entertaining themselves
in a variety of energetic, and often violent, pastimes,
ranging from pillow fights to wrestling.

"You survived your first day?"

"Oh, more or less, yes. The only problem is, I spent so

long cleaning up in the chem lab that I managed to miss dinner."

"Well, that would explain why you survived. The food here is pretty dangerous stuff. It was toad-in-the-hole today, allegedly. But I think actual toads would have been much less awful."

Daphne smiled, despite Veronica's face showing no sign that she had been joking.

"All right, you lot—two minutes!" yelled Marion from her four-poster. "And no flashlights after lights-out tonight. Save your batteries for . . . er, for emergencies, all right? Jolly good. Come on, now. Everybody tuck yourselves in and straight off to sleep."

Daphne closed her disguised copy of *Scarlet Fury* and, with a sigh, tucked it under her bed (on top of the disguised copy of *Daisy's Little Kitten*).

"Is it good, then?" said Veronica doubtfully.

"Oh, it's, er . . . much more exciting than it looks," said Daphne.

"It'd need to be. Night-night."

The girl in the bed nearest the door flicked the light switch and plunged the dorm into darkness.

"Night-night," said Daphne.

There were a few whispers and giggles, quickly

shushed by Marion, but on the whole Daphne was surprised that the girls were so quick to settle down. She had expected at least a small riot, but instead it seemed that everyone was going obediently to sleep. Perhaps, she thought, they were worn out from all their misbehavior throughout the day. It must be exhausting, she thought, although she herself was quite tired enough, even though she'd been good.

She snuggled down and hugged Edgar Rabbit to her face, his fur against her skin comforting and familiar, with the faintest trace of her mother's perfume. In the darkness and quiet, she could almost imagine she was in bed at home. She closed her eyes tight, rubbed her cheek against the worn fuzziness of Edgar's muzzle, felt the world dissolving away, and drifted happily to sleep.

In her dream, Daphne was at the seaside, on the beach, on a beautiful sunny day, and had just built an elaborate sandcastle. It had turrets, windows, battlements, even a drawbridge made from a washed-up piece of sea-smoothed wooden plank, and an intricate network of moats encircled the whole thing.

Daphne stood back from her handiwork and nodded. It was truly magnificent.

She reached up to plant a flag in the top of the castle, but now it had grown: It was as tall as Daphne—taller— blocking out the sun. She stretched up, straining to reach high enough, standing on tiptoes, wet sand between her toes. She was close to toppling, but she could just reach high enough. Then, as she pressed the wooden shaft of the flag down into the sand, the castle began to tremble.

At first it was just a tiny movement, barely notice- able except that it sent trickles of sand flowing down the sides of the castle. Then the tremor grew, and the trickles became tor- rents. Then Daphne felt the vibrations herself, rising up from the ground, running through her body. She was shaken from her tiptoe pose and stum- bled backward, staring at the sandcastle as cracks raced through it, down from the flag. The ground bucked beneath Daphne's feet, the castle crumbled to nothing before her, and her body shook and shook and—

"Hey! Wake up!"

"Aaargh!" said Daphne, opening her eyes to find a blinding light shining straight into them. She clamped them shut again and threw up a hand for good measure.

"Hoy! Hands off, Erica, you little brute! And point the flashlight away from her face, you silly ass!"

"Sorreeee," said Erica, the owner of the first voice, sounding not sorry at all.

Daphne opened her eyes again, and blinked away a

flurry of stars until she could see straight. Behind Erica, who, it turned out, had a sour face that matched her voice very well, was Marion, standing in a purposeful pose, like an intrepid explorer about to trek into the jungle or cross a desert (albeit in checkered pajamas and a comfy dressing gown).

"What ho, Daffers!" she said, in a sort of roared whisper. "Come on, then. Up and at 'em!"

Daphne sat up.

"Eh? But it's not morning, surely . . . ?"

She became blearily aware of a low buzz of activity around the dorm as girls got out of bed and scrabbled in drawers for flashlights or pulled on dressing gowns.

"Surprise!" said Veronica, springing out of the next bed. "Midnight feast!"

"Ancient tradition," said Marion. "New girls always get one. So shake a leg!"

Daphne raised herself onto an elbow and blearily squinted at the alarm clock by her bed.

"Midnight feast?" she said. "But it's not even half past ten."

"Ah yes," Marion said. "Element of surprise, you see. So: Socks or slippers, all right? No shoes. Don't want the

Roar hearing you clumping about on our way to the larder, do we?"

"I suppose not, but, really, there's no need to go to any trouble on my—"

"Oh, shut up and get up!" said Erica, poking Daphne hard with a bony finger.

"Ow!" said Daphne, and swung her legs round to sit on the edge of her bed. "All right, all right."

She fumbled on her dressing gown and looked under her bed for her slippers.

"Originally we'd had it planned for *last* night, of course," said Marion.

"Oh, but then I didn't arrive, so you put it off."

"Oh, no, we did it anyway. The girls were all keyed up for it; couldn't call it off. Now we're doing your one. Erica said it was a stupid idea. Said we'd be pushing our luck doing two nights in a row. But Ronnie Keyhole suggested we just change the time. Jolly clever."

"Ronnie Keyhole? Oh, Veronica."

"That's right." Grinning, Veronica appeared at Marion's side. "But we should get a move on or it *will* be a midnight feast after all by the time we get to the larder."

"Quite right," said Marion. "Come on, then, troops. Let's be off."

Veronica and Daphne joined the back of the line.

"Thanks," said Daphne. "For persuading them to go ahead with it, I mean."

"You're welcome. Oh, hey, have you got a flashlight?"

"Oh! No. No, I haven't."

"I'll grab my spare. You go on ahead, and I'll catch up." Veronica turned back to her bed.

"Well, be quick about it," said Marion. "Come on, Daffers, you stick with me." Marion followed Daphne out and, careful to make no noise, shut the door behind her.

The girls moved on in near silence and very little light. Erica, at the head of the throng, and Marion, at the rear, made sparing use of their flashlights to light the way for the others, but Daphne deduced that everyone else was expected to do without. They made slow, careful progress down the stairs as a result, but they were impressively stealthy. Even Marion was quiet, Daphne noted with surprise.

"Here you are," whispered Veronica, who, it turned out, was even quieter, appearing seemingly from nowhere at Daphne's side as they neared the foot of the stairs. Daphne had to hold in a yelp of surprise, and then the effort nearly made her giggle. Veronica grinned as she handed over a flashlight, and Daphne smiled her thanks. Then Veronica pointed to her toy kangaroo, whose head was poking out of her satchel.

"I brought RooRoo along, too. For luck."

As they stepped down from the last step, the column of girls came to a halt. They were still and silent for a moment, then Erica, at the head of the crowd, pointed her flashlight at the ceiling and flashed it twice, and Marion's face relaxed.

"All clear," she said, and gave Daphne a smile as flashlights flickered on throughout the group.

Veronica turned hers on, too, and pointed to the one she'd given to Daphne.

"That one's a bit tricky," she said. "Dodgy wiring, I suppose. But it's better than nothing."

"Thanks."

Daphne flicked the switch, but nothing happened.

"Give it a whack."

Daphne slapped it into the palm of her other hand, and the light came on.

"There you go," said Veronica. "You've got the magic touch."

The crowd set off along the corridor, their flashlight beams playing over their surroundings like searchlights. The girls stayed mostly quiet, but there was a more

relaxed, playful atmosphere now, with some excited whispering and giggling as they went along. Daphne giggled, too, and realized that, rather to her surprise, she was enjoying herself, enjoying the thrill of sneaking about in the dark: the sense of danger on the one hand, but the comfort of being part of a gang on the other. That sense of belonging was a help, too, whenever she imagined that she heard soft footsteps up ahead, or when some innocent piece of furniture was momentarily transformed, by imagination and swaying flashlights, into a looming shadowy threat. Daphne felt as if her heart was dancing wildly—stopping one moment, racing with excitement the next—but somehow it was thrilling rather than scary.

She looked over at Veronica, expecting to see these feelings reflected in her face, but was surprised by her somber expression.

"You look very serious." She gave Veronica a playful nudge.

Veronica's face snapped into a warm grin. "Sorry, I was miles away."

"Oh. Were you thinking about your uncle?"

"What?" Veronica looked shocked.

"You said this morning . . . You'd had a letter? Some bad news?"

"Oh. Oh, yes. I'd forgotten I'd mentioned that. Thought you were a mind reader for a second."

"Well, actually, yes. Didn't I mention that?" Daphne giggled. "The power of my mind is beyond the understanding of science, don't you know? Actually, I—"

Daphne's flashlight buzzed and flickered.

"Oh." Daphne gave it a shake, which only made it worse.

"Maybe that's your brain waves interfering with it!" said Veronica.

"Or maybe it just needs another whack," said Daphne. She gave it another whack. It went out completely. "Oops. Sorry, I think I killed it."

Veronica shrugged happily in reply. "It had it coming. You'd better get yourself a new one in the village over the weekend. Oh, but get your name scratched onto it as soon as you do or you won't keep it long in this place."

"So," said Daphne as they crept past the doors to the dining hall, "how will we get into the larder? Won't it be locked?"

"Oh yes," said Veronica. "There's a new padlock on the door ever since the third years' last raid. They cleared the place out, silly fools. We'd been picking the old lock and taking bits and bobs now and again quite happily for months, and no one noticed. Then the threes messed it up for the lot of us. Mrs. McKay was livid."

"So how *are* we going to get in?"

"Oh, well, obviously we've dug a tunnel since then," said Marion, who had come to a halt. "Well, Nelly did, didn't you, Nelly?"

A fresh-faced girl at Marion's side gave a modest shrug.

"A . . . tunnel? Really? You're joking, aren't you?"

"I never joke about tunnels," said Marion, adopting her most serious of serious faces. "Show her your handiwork, Nell."

Nelly crouched down to pull aside a rug on the floor. Then she put a finger through a knothole in one of the floorboards and pulled, opening a trapdoor that, until then, had been entirely undetectable.

"That's amazing!" said Daphne, and Nelly gave a smile of quiet pride.

Marion turned to Erica and nodded her head toward the trapdoor. Erica nodded back, gripped her flashlight in her teeth, and lowered herself into the hole.

Daphne peered down into it. There was a metal ladder leading straight into the darkness.

"Crikey! It goes quite deep, doesn't it?"

"Oh yes. She's a jolly diligent tunneler, is Nelly.

Insisted you should be able to stand up straight in it, you see."

"And . . ." Daphne frowned at the dancing spotlight of Erica's flashlight as she descended. "And you wallpapered the insides?"

"Of course!" said Nelly. "I haven't had time to put the pictures up yet, though." She sounded faintly ashamed. "One of the fifth years has done us some fake Monets. It's going to look lovely."

Deep beneath the floor, the distant light of Erica's flashlight disappeared from view. Daphne looked about her to see who was going next, but no one seemed to be making any move toward the entrance.

"Right," whispered Marion. "Lights out, girls."

The flashlights went out. The darkness was thick and full, and now all talking ceased and everyone was still. In the darkness and silence, even though she knew there were more than a dozen other girls around her, Daphne suddenly felt very alone. Alone and rather frightened.

There was a clock somewhere down the corridor— a big old grandfather clock, which she remembered passing—ticking relentlessly away, counting off each long second. It was a small sound, but it resounded down the corridor, magnified by the night.

Daphne counted the seconds, which grew into minutes, and more minutes, and all the while her nervousness grew. What was she doing here? If she was caught out of her dorm, on her first night, imagine the trouble she would be in! And after the "incident" at her last school . . . Her father had said how lucky she had been to get in at St. Rita's "under the circumstances." He would never forgive her if she made a mess of things.

She wished that she had just stayed in bed and never come out on this silly jaunt. She didn't really know any of these girls properly. And she couldn't even see them now. She listened for them, trying to discern a breath,

a murmur, a shuffling foot, but all there was was the
ticking of the clock.

Then, in the absolute dark that surrounded Daphne,
there appeared a small square that was not quite so
dark. She watched it, and it grew fractionally brighter,
and she realized that she was looking at the entrance to
the tunnel, and that Erica was returning, her flashlight
beam preceding her, lighting her way.

Marion turned on her flashlight and pointed the
beam at the open trapdoor.

"Daffers," she hissed. "Help her out, will you?"

Daphne nodded and tip-
toed over. She knelt down
as she heard the soft
rhythm of Erica's slip-
pered feet ascending
the ladder. A hand
appeared up from the
hole, waving a glass
jar. Daphne took it
from her and glanced
at the label.

"Black currant jam?" she
said. She looked back to Erica emerging from the tunnel.

"Is that it?" she whispered. "All this trouble for one jar of jam?"

Her ravenous stomach rumbled its disappointment.

"Steady there, Tiger!" said Marion. "Thing is, most of the food in there is just awful, so we don't want to pinch that. And, well, we snaffled most of the good stuff yesterday. This is more of a token gesture, old girl. For the sake of tradition, don't you know."

"But if we're only getting *this*, why did we all need to come along?"

"Well, it's a nice trip out, isn't it?"

"A nice t–trip out?" stuttered Daphne. "But what if we get . . . Hey, leave some for me!"

Erica had opened the jar, and all the girls were crowding in to scoop up a fingerful and eat it.

"Play the game, girls," said Marion. "Daffers is guest of honor at the feast, after all."

The girls parted, licking their sticky lips, to reveal Erica holding the almost-empty jar.

"Oops," said Erica, with no remorse, and held up the jar toward Daphne.

"Thanks a lot." Daphne wiped a finger around the inside of the jar and gathered up a faint smear of jam, then dipped her finger into her mouth and licked it clean.

Oh, but it was good! It was sweet and sharp and utterly delicious, and made all the more so by Daphne's hunger. She couldn't help letting out a soft sigh of appreciation.

"Shh!" Veronica tapped an urgent finger on Daphne's shoulder, and Daphne obediently shushed, just as Erica and Marion turned off their flashlights and plunged them back into total darkness. Daphne held her breath and listened for whatever had put Veronica on the alert. But all she could hear was the ticking of the clock, echoing down the corridor.

Then, as the seconds passed, it seemed that the echo of the clock's ticking got louder. Not only that, but it fell out of time with the ticking, growing clearer, more distinct, until it revealed itself to be another sound altogether: the sound of approaching footsteps. Steps taken by feet wearing important-sounding shoes.

"The Roar!" hissed Marion. "Run! Every girl for herself! Back to the dorm, into bed, no noise, no lights. Quick as you like!"

The sound of swiftly padding feet dissolved into the velvet darkness, leaving Daphne alone.

Thanks a bunch! she thought.

Daphne stood motionless, as if paralyzed, but her mind was racing. She held down the bubbling panic she felt rising in her stomach and assessed her situation, scanning round for inspiration. But all she could see was the approaching beam of a flashlight; all she could hear was the marching footsteps growing louder, coming down the corridor.

Daphne knew the way back to the dorm, and safety, but it led past the Roar. The other girls had run off the other way. Daphne could follow, blindly, but she would have no idea where she was going. Her best hope was to hide and let Cynthia pass—but where?

The scything flashlight beam advanced. Daphne backed away, squinting into the darkness, searching frantically for somewhere to hide herself, but finding nothing.

Then her heart jolted as her foot found the edge of the entrance to the tunnel. Another inch or so, and she would have toppled in. She dropped down, braced herself with one hand on either side of the hole, and lowered herself down. One scrabbling foot found a rung of the ladder, then the other.

She glanced back down the corridor, saw the flashlight beam on the grandfather clock and the dim figure of Cynthia stooping to peer through the window of one of the classroom doors. Daphne fumbled for the trapdoor and grabbed its edge just as Cynthia straightened and began to swing the flashlight round. The light hit the far wall just as Daphne pulled at the trapdoor. Cynthia's footsteps drummed louder, and the flashlight beam swung toward Daphne. She crouched and pulled the trapdoor closed over her head just before the light hit it.

She held herself perfectly still on the ladder, swallowing her breath as the outline of the trapdoor lit up above her and then dissolved into deep blackness. Two more footsteps and then ... nothing.

Motionless in the quiet dark, Daphne imagined she could hear Cynthia's breath somewhere above her. The trapdoor creaked. Cynthia was standing right on it. Why didn't she just move on? The trapdoor creaked again as Cynthia shifted her weight. Daphne gulped. What if she saw the rug! She would surely wonder why. Then she might discover the trapdoor, and Daphne would—

"Who's there?" shouted Cynthia.

Daphne winced.

"Is that you, Bullmore? Hey! Hey, wait there, you little . . ."

There was a drumroll of footsteps, running away down the corridor and quickly fading, then beautiful, beautiful silence.

Daphne blew out a long-held breath and drew in a fresh one. She offered silent thanks to whichever of the girls was Bullmore, then carefully opened the trapdoor just a crack. She was peeping out round the half-open lid when she heard something. A distant thud? Perhaps a cry? It was too indistinct to be sure. But then there were footsteps, and a flicker of dancing light at the far end of the corridor.

"Oh, dash it!"

Daphne lowered her head back down and closed the trapdoor. She listened, trembling, as the dull rumble of footsteps passed overhead and began to fade. Daphne gulped in a luxuriant breath, then blew it slowly out. She raised a hand to the door.

More footsteps.

"Oh, for heaven's sake!" Daphne hissed to herself.

Then a voice, so quiet at first that Daphne wasn't even sure she hadn't imagined it, then louder, dispelling her doubt, calling out what seemed to be a single word, though Daphne couldn't make out what it was. Daphne stood, still and silent at the top of the ladder, eyes closed in the darkness, straining to hear.

There was the voice again: the same muffled word, nothing more. Then, after a moment, the boards of the hatch creaking as someone stepped onto it. Then, amidst the noise of her breath and her racing heart, she could just pick out the softest murmur of urgent whispered conversation.

Even standing just beneath the hatch, she could not make out what was being said, but it seemed there were two voices, and neither speaker was happy. Then the hatch creaked as there was a brief, drunken dance of shuffled, scuffling steps. There was a sharp cry, then a thump on the trapdoor that made Daphne's heart lurch.

Then there was silence.

Daphne stood tensed on the ladder, her face turned up toward the hatch, her eyes wide, as if trying to stare through the darkness and the wood of the trapdoor. Her shallow breaths rasped in the quiet; her hands clasped the ladder achingly tight. She listened hard, and heard nothing, nothing, and more nothing.

Eventually she convinced herself that surely whoever had been up there must be gone. She adjusted her slippered feet on their rung and reached up, ready to push open the hatch. Her breath was still and tense in her throat, her every nerve tingling.

Something fell onto her face. Warm and wet. A single drop of liquid hitting her cheek. She flinched with the tiny shock of it, jerked like a sprung mousetrap, and first one foot, then the other slid from the rung. For a split second Daphne felt as if she were floating—as if she might just reach out and retake her place on the ladder. Then her heart lurched, as gravity took hold of her and flung her down, down into the dark.

Everything in Daphne's head was fuzzy. Then, when she opened her eyes, the darkness was fuzzy, too. She lay still, waiting for her thoughts to settle, trying to remember where she was and how she had gotten there. She thought she had just woken, but had she fainted or been knocked out? She wasn't sure. And if she had, how long had she been unconscious? There was no way of knowing. So she lay there for a moment in the unknowable darkness, enjoying the certainty of the floor beneath her.

Then she stood, woozily, fumbled for the ladder and took hold of it, steadying herself. She listened for a moment. Reassured by the silence, she climbed to the top, listened again, and opened up the hatch just a fraction, drawing a narrow line of gray in the blackness. Hearing the faint ticking of the clock, but nothing more, she pushed open the trapdoor completely, hauled herself up out of the tunnel, and stood for a moment, drinking in the silence.

She drew in a long breath, faintly scented with lavender from the bushes outside, then slowly let it go in a grateful sigh. She felt more alert now, her head flushed clearer by the air. She shut the hatch, groped in the dark for the rug, pulled it back into place, then hurried off quietly back toward the dorm.

Daphne had half expected there to be trouble waiting for her when she got back, but when she reached the landing she was relieved to see that there was no light coming under the door. If anyone had been caught out, then it looked as if her share of the trouble could wait until morning at least.

Someone needs to oil those hinges! thought Daphne as she crept in and tried to close the door behind her without creaking. But Marion's snoring drowned out the noise, and no one stirred in their bed.

That's all right, girls; don't lose any sleep worrying about the new girl, will you?

There was just enough moonlight through the thin material of the curtains to see that all the beds were occupied, so it seemed no one had been caught. Daphne tiptoed carefully round the hole in the floor, shed her dressing gown, and threw back the covers on her bed. Her eyelids were already drooping as she climbed in. She snuggled down, grateful for the welcoming embrace of the bedclothes, and then closed her eyes, emptied her mind, and fell into a deep, exhausted sleep.

TWELVE

They were awoken early the next morning by a commotion. And while the pupils of St. Rita's School for Spirited Girls were, on the whole, pretty familiar with commotions, they usually preferred them to be of their own making and conducted at a civilized hour of the day. This commotion, whatever it was, was in the other dorms farther along the corridor. But as Daphne and the other fourth years blearily awoke, they could tell that it was heading their way.

"Hey ho," said Marion. "Something's up."

"Sounds like trouble!" said Erica.

"What's going on?" said Daphne.

Miss Bagley, looking as if she had dressed in rather a hurry, burst through the door.

"Everybody up! Emergency assembly in the main hall in five minutes. Unimaginable punishments for anyone who's late."

She shot a look around the room.

"Too many bodies still in bed. Get moving. Now!"

Then she was back out in the corridor, heading toward the next dorm, calling back to them through the open door: "Unimaginable punishments!"

Marion rose huffing from her four-poster and slid an arm into her dressing gown with no great sense of urgency. She caught Daphne's eye and gave her a grin.

"What ho, Daffers! Am I pleased to see you. Didn't hear you getting back last night. Thought maybe the Roar had got hold of you. Sorry you got left behind. Bit stinky of me, that. Ashamed to say I panicked a bit. Most of us hightailed it up the west staircase. It's out of bounds on account of it being unsafe, but if you know what you're doing you can still get up it. Tricky business in the dark, mind, even if you're used to it. Jolly impressed you could manage it on your first night."

"Oh, I didn't go up it," said Daphne as she continued to

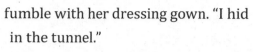

fumble with her dressing gown. "I hid in the tunnel."

"Well! There's quick thinking." Marion gave an appreciative nod. "You're a cool one, Daphne B. Cool as a cucumber, but nothing like so green, that's you."

"Thanks," said Daphne, whose attempts to rearrange her half-inside-out dressing gown had only succeeded in turning it fully inside out. She decided to give it up as a bad job and put it on that way. "But what do you think this assembly's about?"

"Search me, old girl," said Marion.

"I hope they haven't found the tunnel," muttered Erica, casting a dark look in Daphne's direction.

"Well, I closed the door and put the rug back over it . . . after you'd all run off." Daphne gave Erica a defiant stare.

Erica scowled back at her. She rubbed a finger against Daphne's cheek, then held it up to her to show a smudge of dark red on its tip.

"Whatever it's about," said Erica, "you'd better not turn up with jam on your face, had you?"

Daphne gave her a puzzled look.

"But I didn't . . ."

She wiped a hand over her cheek and examined it, but there was nothing more there.

"What . . . ?" she began, but Erica was already making her way out the door, with Marion right behind her.

"Come on, Daffers," called Marion. "Shake a leg or you'll miss all the fun."

Daphne hurried after her, hopping past the hole in the floor as she put on her second slipper.

There was quite a crush on the stairs. Tributary streams of girls from the various dorms combined at the top of the staircase, forming one mighty torrent of children gushing down to the ground floor. A few were in full uniform, but most had simply grabbed a pinafore or blazer and flung it on over the top of their nightdress or pajamas. Some of the younger girls clutched teddy bears, hugging them close to protect them from the surrounding horde. A few of the more eager pupils bypassed the crowd by sliding down the banisters.

Daphne, though, was not at all impatient to get to the hall. The more she thought about it, the more certain she became that the assembly must surely be connected to the events of the previous night, and she was about to get into a great deal of trouble. And she really didn't want to be in trouble again. As she approached the door to the main hall, she began to consider the possibility of not going in at all. Perhaps she could just run off and start a new life somewhere. A train to the coast and then stowaway on a ferry to the continent. Or if she could get to America somehow . . .

"Wake up, Daffers. If you keep dawdling, you'll miss the start."

Marion slapped her on the back with such force that Daphne was propelled through the doorway and into the hall. The last few girls were finding places to sit, but otherwise the entire school was assembled on the benches and rows of chairs. A buzz of anticipation charged the air.

"What a to-do, eh? Wonder what it's all about. Reckon someone must really be in for it." Marion adopted an expression of grave

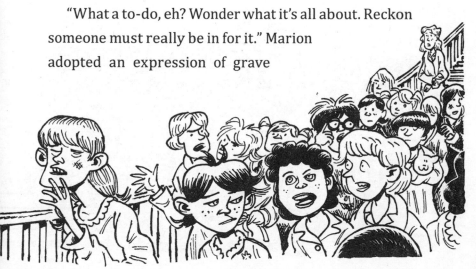

thoughtfulness that lasted for about half a second before giving way to a more long-lasting grin. "Come on, let's get front-row seats. We don't want to miss anything."

She towed Daphne, too appalled to speak, forward, past the older girls on chairs at the back and around to the center of the front bench, where the first years sat. Daphne glanced up at the members of staff assembling on the stage at the front of the hall. Even in her preoccupied state, she was briefly distracted by the presence of a nun amongst them, but otherwise mostly all she saw was their feet, as she kept her head down. But the teachers' footwear alone was enough to show her that the staff, too, had arrived in a hurry, judging by all the loose shoelaces and odd socks.

"Special treat for you, girls," said Marion to a pair of goggle-eyed little 'uns. "You are temporarily promoted to the hallowed ranks of the fourth years. Off you pop."

After a brief gawp, they popped off, and Daphne (in stunned silence) and Marion (chuckling contentedly) took their places, comically tall amongst their younger neighbors, standing out like buck teeth.

"There," said Marion. "That's better."

Daphne felt very strongly that it was not better at all. In fact it was very much worse. She would rather be sitting hidden from view on the back row of chairs amidst the sixth years. Or better yet, not be there at all. She thought, again, about running away. Perhaps *South America*. Maybe someplace like Bolivia . . .

"You will be quiet *now* please, girls!" shouted Miss Bagley, striding onto the stage. "And for heaven's sake, sit down, George!"

Daphne turned her head to see George, even more disheveled than he had been the day before, dithering at the side of the hall. He scanned the benches and chairs for a space to sit, then, with a shrug, sank down to park himself cross-legged on the floor.

"Right, then," said Miss Bagley, and the edge in her voice was enough to gain everyone's silent attention.

She prowled the stage, strafing her rapt audience with a stare that could have felled trees. There was nothing about her now of the kindly friend that she had seemed in her office.

"Let's see if we can get this little matter sorted out quickly, and then maybe . . ."

She came to a halt center stage, leaning forward as if examining each pupil minutely.

". . . just maybe . . ."

Every girl (and George, too) held their breath.

". . . none of you need end up in prison."

Daphne made a weird squeaking noise that was mercifully drowned out by the simultaneous gasping of every other girl in the hall. In the moment of shocked silence that followed, Daphne began to compose in her head a defense of her actions the previous night. Maybe, she thought, if she could come up with something good enough, she might just avoid being expelled, or indeed arrested. *Maybe I could blame it all on Erica*, she thought. *After all, she was the only one who had actually stolen anything. I might be in trouble with the school, but at least I haven't committed an actual crime.*

But then she remembered the fingerful of jam she had eaten.

"Receiving stolen goods!" she whispered to herself, though not so quietly that Marion didn't give her a quizzical glance.

Daphne peeked up at Miss Bagley and was relieved to find that she had been distracted by something at the back of the hall.

Daphne turned to see that a fifth-year girl had clamped her hand over her neighbor's mouth and was trying to prevent her from raising her hand. A second later, the two of them wrestled each other off their chairs and disappeared from view, though it seemed clear from the cries and yells (and occasional sightings of a raised fist) that whatever their disagreement, they were not settling it by peaceful means. As Daphne looked on, she heard a dull gentle impact on the floor by the stage, then saw an athletic-looking member of staff (the gym teacher, she presumed) race down the side of the hall and leap into the baying mob of spectators that had by now formed around the ongoing conflict. She soon emerged, hauling the offending pair by their collars to the side of the room.

"It was 'er what done it!" said the first girl. "She dug up them rosebushes."

"Yurr, I done that," said the second. "But she's the one what sold 'em."

She aimed a kick at the other girl, but the gym teacher's grip kept her just out of range. "And you ain't even paid me my share!"

A sharp, strong yank pulled each of them momentarily off their feet and shocked them into silent obedience.

"Thank you, Miss Trowel," said Miss Bagley from the stage. "Ahem . . . the matter in hand is nothing to do with rosebushes. It is, in fact—"

"They made me do it, miss! It wasn't my fault!"

Miss Bagley rolled her eyes.

"Nor is it about the kidnapping of the milkman's horse, Maude," she sighed. "So please be quiet. Though, since we're on the subject, yes, we do know all about that. No, I mean—"

"Oh Lord! It's not about the gin distillery in the cellar, is it, miss?" This from one of the sixth years, quickly shushed by her neighbors.

"*Is* there a gin distillery in the cellar, Martina?" Miss Bagley looked surprised.

"Er, absolutely not, miss," said Martina.

"I am very glad to hear it. Now," Miss Bagley shouted, both hands raised in front of her, "if you'll all just *stop* confessing for a moment . . . Good. It appears that there was a very unfortunate incident last night."

Daphne gulped. It seemed very loud to her. It was a wonder that everyone wasn't staring at her.

"There was a break-in," said Miss Bagley.

Perhaps everyone is *staring at me*, thought Daphne. *Maybe that's why I suddenly feel so hot. Everyone's eyes burning into me.*

"And as if that wasn't bad enough . . . Cynthia, would you join me, please?"

"Oh Lord!" muttered Daphne. She gazed down at the ground. Panic fluttered in her chest.

Then the rest of the girls all gasped, even louder than before, and Daphne looked up to see Cynthia Rawlinson with a black eye and her arm in a sling.

Well, she thought, *at least* that's *someone else's fault and not mine.*

A shrill cry rang out from the back of the hall.

"What on *earth* is going on?"

Daphne turned her head and recognized the woman clattering toward the stage as the one she had glimpsed the day before through the open door of her office.

"Crikey!" whispered Marion. "Mrs. McKay, out of her office and on public display! Today is just full of surprises! And it's not even breakfast time yet."

She was a tall, spindly woman, dressed rather haphazardly, and she stomped forward, wearing an expression that combined irritation and bemusement.

"Miss Bagley, can you please explain to me why you have assembled the entire school here without even informing me?" She climbed up the steps at the side of the stage. "And furthermore . . . Oh my goodness! Cynthia, my poor child! Whatever has happened to you?"

"I'm sorry, Headmistress," said Miss Bagley quietly, then continued in a voice loud enough to be heard by the whole hall, "but there has been a serious incident, as you can see, and I felt I had to act at once. As I was about to tell the girls: Last night, Cynthia here was woken by a noise somewhere on the ground floor."

Oh crikey! thought Daphne.

"When she came down to investigate—you said you heard another noise, didn't you, Cynthia?"

"Yes, miss. From the library."

"Someone had broken into the library," Miss Bagley continued. "Cynthia was outside the door when they came out, and was knocked down the steps. Mr. Thanet found her unconscious in the corridor this morning as he was cleaning. He took her to Matron, and luckily nothing's broken."

"Thank goodness!" said Mrs. McKay. "And, Cynthia, dear, did you see who was responsible?"

"Well, they were tall, but apart from that . . . It was very dark, so . . ."

"No? Oh dear." Mrs. McKay turned to face the ranks of girls seated in the hall, though she seemed somewhat reluctant to look directly at them. "Now then, girls. I want whoever it was who hurt poor Cynthia here to own up now, please."

"Ha! Fat chance!" muttered Marion, and this sentiment seemed to capture the mood of the room, judging by the gentle hum of giggling that started up. Even Miss Bagley rolled her eyes. Certainly no one volunteered themselves as the culprit.

"I'm afraid it's rather more serious than that, Headmistress. I'm not sure it *was* one of the girls. Someone may have broken in from outside the school. So I'm afraid, unless any of the girls can tell us otherwise, that we had better call the police."

"The police?" spluttered Mrs. McKay. "Nonsense! I'm . . . I'm sure there's no need for that." She turned to Cynthia. "No bones broken, you say?"

"Well, no, miss." Cynthia winced as she spoke. "But—"

"There you are, then. And, Miss Bagley, what evidence do you have of anyone breaking in from outside?"

"Well, none yet. But there was a window open, so there'd be no need to—"

"No evidence. I see." She gave Miss Bagley a withering look. "An unfortunate accident, to be sure, and we

will get to the bottom of it. But I'm sure the police have better things to do than investigate the tomfoolery of our girls. And besides, we have a very important lacrosse game against St. Walter's tomorrow. We can't have today's practice disrupted by police running all over the place, can we? Now . . ."

She turned again to face her audience.

"I daresay that whoever it was who was larking about in the library last night and caused poor Cynthia to take a tumble is feeling really quite embarrassed and foolish and very, very sorry about it, so I won't ask you to reveal yourself to the rest of the school. But I'm afraid I must *insist* that you make yourself known to me before . . . well, before the end of the week, shall we say? Yes. Or else there will be—well, I'm afraid there will be very serious consequences."

"Is that it?" whispered Daphne.

"About par for the course, old girl," said Marion.

Miss Bagley looked appalled.

"Now off you all go and—"

"With respect, Headmistress," Miss Bagley butted in, turning Mrs. McKay's face to stone. Miss Bagley lowered her voice, no longer addressing the assembly as a whole, but still clearly audible to Daphne sitting rapt in the front row. "I don't think you quite understand the seriousness of the situation. I don't think this is just *larking about*, Agatha. And if it wasn't one of the girls . . . if someone broke in, then—"

"Broke in?" hissed Mrs. McKay. "To go to the library? Ridiculous. It's just one of the girls being silly. Youthful high spirits, albeit rather misdirected."

She turned to the girls again and raised her voice.

"Have no fear, Miss Bagley, I shall find the culprit, and I shall have stern words with her. Very stern words indeed. But, really, all this . . . *fuss* was quite unnecessary. Now, girls, this is most unfortunate, of course, but we must not leap to conclusions. I shall assess all the facts of the matter coolly and calmly once I've had the opportunity to speak with poor Cynthia. In the meantime, get dressed, and we'll all get on with the business of the day, shall we? And remember, lacrosse players: You are all excused from your usual lessons today for extra training with Miss Trowel. But do please try not to hospitalize each other. Thank you. Thank you."

The girls began to rise and shuffle out of the hall, as did the staff—all but Mrs. McKay and Miss Bagley, who remained on the stage in animated but whispered dispute.

THIRTEEN

As they left the hall, George grabbed Daphne by the arm.

"Come on," he said, raising his voice over the chatter of the crowd. "Library."

"But I need to get dressed. And then I'm going to my history lesson," said Daphne.

"No, you're not. Don't be so ridiculous."

"But I like history!"

"So do I, up to a point. Mrs. Quigley, on the other hand, hates it. Or at least you'd think so from her lessons. She's about as inspiring as a sock, that woman.

And besides, the bell for first lesson is still more than an hour off. Mmm . . . Miss Bagley got us up early, remember. It's not even time for breakfast yet."

Daphne made a brief show of feigning indifference, but it was very unconvincing.

"As inspiring as a sock, you say?" she said.

"Yes," said George. "And not even a stripy one either. A really boring beige sock. With a hole in it."

"Oh, well, in that case . . ." Daphne smiled.

"Come on," said George. "Your library needs you. The door's been forced, books scattered everywhere, and the Lime is predictably furious about it all. It's quite entertaining, actually. And, as a probationary assistant assistant, it's your duty to help clean up."

"Or it will be, once Emily Lime writes it into my contract," sighed Daphne. "All right, then."

"That's the spirit!" said George, and they set off together, their excited chatter feeding into the hubbub of the crowd around them.

"Are the police here yet?" said Emily Lime at the sound of the door opening. "I want them to check for fingerprints as soon as possible so we can start tidying up."

"Police?" laughed George. "You're joking, aren't you? Mmm . . . Miss Bagley was keen, but I don't think Mrs. McKay could have been persuaded unless the Roar had *at least* been murdered—"

"The Roar?" said Emily Lime. "Never mind about her, what about my library? It's an outrage! Whoever broke in here and ransacked the place, I want them . . . I want them arrested, and tried, and then . . . then sentenced to be hanged, drawn, and quartered!"

She paused, considering what she had just said, and frowned.

"Actually," she said, "forget the trial, just hang, draw, and quarter them straightaway."

"Well, I think Mrs. Mac was more thinking of giving them lines to write—not that they'll ever be caught. You know what she's like; she doesn't want any fuss. And she wants the police to visit here *less* often, so she's hardly likely to invite them here herself."

George took a look around.

"And the library has hardly been *ransacked*, has it? It's just been . . . untidied."

"They broke in!" said Emily Lime. "And they did *not take proper care* while handling the books! It's an outrage!"

"Much worse than murder," whispered George.

131

Daphne examined the wreckage. "Did they take anything?"

"Yes," said George, waving a hand to indicate the library as a whole. "Haven't you noticed? All the books have disappeared!" He adopted a pantomime expression of appalled horror. "Oh, no, wait . . . we didn't have any to begin with."

"I don't know how you can be so flippant," growled Emily Lime. "This is very serious! And whoever is responsible—"

"Why don't we give you a bit of a hand tidying up?" said Daphne. "Then we can see more easily if there's anything missing."

They were standing by the crime section, where three of the shelves had been almost emptied, their books lying scattered about the floor. Daphne knelt down, picked up one of them, and glanced at its spine.

"*Night of the Panther Lady,*" she said, reading the title, "*A Smeeton Westerby Mystery*"—her speech slowed and her eyes widened in surprise as she recognized the name—"by J. H. Buchanan. Oh!"

Daphne turned the book in her hands to view the front cover.

"Oh!" she said again, and recoiled in shock at the Panther Lady's clothing. "Good gracious!"

George took it from her.

"Blimey!" he said. "That's . . . um . . . That poor girl will catch her death of cold!"

He carried on staring at it.

Daphne picked up another book.

"*Killer's Valentine: A Smeeton Westerby Mystery*, by J. H. Buchanan."

And another.

"*Fatal Charm: A Smeeton Westerby Mystery*, by J. H. Buchanan."

Daphne offered the books up to George, but he hadn't finished being outraged by the Panther Lady and didn't

notice, so she passed them to Emily Lime instead.

"Um, are they all ...?"

"Yes," said Emily Lime. "A complete set. One hundred and thirty-seven books. If they've all survived this ... this *outrage*."

Then she started to shelve the books as Daphne passed them up, which seemed to calm her, at least a little. George put the Panther Lady in her place and started helping, too, and they made fast progress at putting everything back in order.

"Well, at least it looks like nothing's been taken," said George after a while. They were down to the last few books now, which they began to slot into the remaining spaces on the shelves.

"No," grumbled Emily Lime. "Well, it was probably just some illiterate girl with a grudge, messing things up out of spite."

"Because," said George, winking at Daphne, "believe it or not, despite her sunny disposition and radiant smile, there are some people who don't much care for our glorious leader here." He tilted his head toward the seething Emily. "Inexplicable, I know, but there it is."

Daphne, lost in thought, did not return his smile.

"I don't understand," she said.

"Really?" said George. "I mean, you have *met* her, so . . ."

"Oh. No, that's not what I meant. The thing is . . . I was downstairs last night. Well, we . . . I probably shouldn't be telling you this, but . . . we all were. The whole fourth year."

"Oh," said George. "Larder raid, was it? That new tunnel of theirs? Jam?"

"Oh. Yes. I thought it was a secret."

"Probably is," said George. "More or less."

"So you lot were crashing about in the corridor," said Emily Lime, "and Cynthia came down to see what all the noise was?"

"Actually, we were all pretty quiet. I don't see how she *could* have heard us."

"Hmm," said George. "Well, her room is more or less above us here. So she was more likely to hear the library being broken into than anything to do with your raid."

"Oh, I see," said Daphne. "But then she had to go the long way round to come down the east staircase, not the rotten west one. Which put us between her and the library."

"Bet she didn't catch anyone, though, did she?" said Emily Lime.

"No. Everyone else ran off, and I hid in the tunnel. Cynthia carried on to the library . . . and the next thing she knew, Mr. Thanet was waking her up on his cleaning rounds this morning. She was unconscious at the bottom of the steps."

"Was she badly hurt?" said Emily Lime.

"A black eye and her arm in a sling—sprained wrist, I reckon," said George. "In quite a lot of pain, it looked like."

"Oh, well, that's something at least," said Emily.

"She'd been out cold all night," said Daphne, giving Emily a dark look. "It could have been very serious!"

"It certainly could," said George. "She's been treated by Matron, so frankly she's lucky to be alive!"

"Whereas," said Emily Lime, her voice trembling, "whoever broke into my library will *wish* they were dead when I get my hands on them! Look! Look what they've done!"

She had replaced the last few books from the floor. Everything was back in place and in order, but on the second shelf up, about a third of the way along, between *Running from Justice* and *Shades of Doubt*, was a gap.

"Ah yes," said George. "Well, actually, that's not *really* missing. At least it hasn't been stolen. At least not last night."

"What are you blathering on about?" said Emily Lime. "It's not here, is it?"

"No. No, it's not. But . . ."

"Then it *is* missing," said Emily Lime.

Daphne thought about the copy of *Scarlet Fury* under her bed. In some ways she thought that now might be a good time to mention it. Not as good a time as the day before, maybe, but better than tomorrow. But she couldn't help wondering what Emily Lime's reaction might be.

"Well, yes, I suppose, in a traditional sense, that would be one way of looking at it," said George, looking increasingly flustered, while Emily Lime looked increasingly infuriated.

Of course the other option, thought Daphne, *rather than yesterday, now, or tomorrow, is never.* And never seemed pretty tempting, just at that moment.

"Certainly it isn't here," George said. "But it's not actually lost. It's . . . um . . ."

Daphne looked at Emily Lime's face. It reminded her of a geography lesson she had once had on the subject of volcanoes. Daphne knew that, for the sake of George, and quite possibly anyone within a five-mile radius, she had better own up.

"It's just that we, er . . . don't know where it is," said George.

Emily Lime began to sputter.

"Oh, well, actually," said Daphne, "we do. I've got that one."

FOURTEEN

I don't understand," George said, already out of breath halfway up the first flight of stairs. "How have *you* got the book if it went missing before you even got here?"

Daphne explained about the porter at the railway station and recalled his description of the woman who had given him the book.

"Ah!" said George. "Short, wide, and in a ratty fur coat. That will have been Mrs. Crump. She must be up and about again, then. That's good."

"And she must have removed the book from school premises without making a note of it in our records," huffed Emily Lime. "That's bad. Disgraceful behavior for a head librarian."

"Well, I don't suppose she meant to," said George. "She did say she was going to read one of the Smeeton Westerbys to *assess their suitability*. It must have been in her room when all her belongings got sent on to her, and included by mistake."

Emily Lime clearly thought that this in no way excused Mrs. Crump, but they had now arrived at the fourth-year dorm, and she didn't pursue the matter. She marched into the room, swinging her head from side to side.

"Right, which one is your bed?"

"I'll get it!" blurted Daphne, pushing past her, then swerving sharply to avoid the hole in the floor. She had been wondering the whole way from the library how she could get the proper cover back onto *Scarlet Fury* without the others noticing, and it hadn't been easy to concentrate with Emily Lime grumbling at her the whole way. Daphne wasn't exactly sure if she was embarrassed that she'd been reading the book, or embarrassed about trying to hide the fact, but she was certain that she didn't want Emily Lime to know. She dived under her bed to deal with the books. Emily Lime stopped to examine the hole in the floor.

"*Another* pogo stick accident?" she said.

"No," said George. "Marion Fink's cannonball. How can you not have heard about that? They were talking about it all over the school for days afterward."

"I wasn't all over the school, was I? I was in the library."

"You really ought to get out more often, you know. Come on, Daffers, you'd better give her the book back. Her Majesty gets twitchy if any of her babies are away for too long."

Daphne, though, had a problem. She crawled out from under the bed and, her face screwed tight with embarrassment, handed a book to Emily Lime.

"What's this?" said Emily Lime.

"It's the missing book," said Daphne.

"*Daisy's Little Kitten*," said Emily Lime, holding it at arm's length between thumb and forefinger. "By Jemima Winthrop-Thwaite?"

"No, no," said Daphne. "It *is Scarlet Fury*, it's just . . . it's just that I swapped the cover with another book. And now the other book's gone missing. But I'm sure I left both of them under my bed last night. Perhaps in all the fuss this morning it got moved, but I don't really see how. Unless somebody . . . stole it."

"Well," said George, "if someone thought they were stealing *Scarlet Fury* and got *Daisy's Little Kitten* instead, then they're in for a heck of a disappointment."

Daphne looked at Emily Lime, who was looking grumpy, but who wasn't shouting at her as she had expected. Daphne wondered if this was a good or a bad thing.

"*Why* did you swap the covers?" said Emily Lime at last.

"Oh," said Daphne. "Well, I was reading it—*Scarlet Fury*, I mean—on the train, and, well, it looks like . . .

a certain sort of book that"—she could feel the heat rising in her cheeks, and she was waving her hands about too much—"that, maybe, I ought not . . . that is, that some people might think I ought not . . ." She decided to put her overactive hands out of the way in her pockets, but this only reminded her that her dressing gown was inside out, so the pockets were currently out of reach.

"You were embarrassed?" said Emily Lime.

"Well, yes."

"You were embarrassed about *reading*?"

"Yes."

Emily Lime looked straight into Daphne's eyes, transfixing her with a disconcerting stare.

"*Never* do that again," said Emily Lime. She looked down at the book, wincing only slightly. "Now, get changed, for heaven's sake, and let's get back."

"I'll make myself scarce," said George, heading for the door, but pointing past Daphne as he went. "Who's the unconvincing sleeping beauty next door, by the way?"

"Eh?" said Daphne. She looked over at the next bed along and saw that its blankets were still draped over a motionless form.

"Veronica?" she said, reaching out with a tentative hand.

Gaining no response, Daphne gave the blankets a gentle nudge; then, when that still brought no response, she pulled back the covers, revealing a pillow and some bundled-up clothes.

"Ah! The old pillow trick," said George as he exited the room. "It's a classic. Though I'm surprised that effort fooled anyone."

"Well," said Daphne, "in all the fuss this morning, I'm not surprised we didn't pay much attention. But I don't see why she did it at all."

"Wasn't it for the larder raid, then?" said George, from the other side of the door.

"No, it wasn't like that when we left the dorm last night. She must have slipped away early this morning. Oh, unless . . . she came back to get me a flashlight after we'd all set off for the raid. She could have done it then, I suppose . . ."

Daphne wriggled an arm free from her dressing gown.

"And she could have taken your book at the same time," said George. "Even if she presumably meant to steal the other one."

"A book thief? The fiend!" said Emily Lime.

"I suppose she could have," said Daphne. "But I don't see why she would."

Now that she had removed her dressing gown, she set about turning it right side out.

"No, she's not what you'd call a keen reader," said George.

Daphne draped the dressing gown over the end of her bed. "And she was acting so . . . What? What are you staring at?"

"Is that jam?" said George. He was pointing at Daphne's dressing gown.

On the front of it, revealed now that it was no longer inside out, were several splotches of red.

"Oh!" said Daphne.

She examined the stains more closely.

"No," said Daphne, turning to face the other two. "I think . . ."

She gulped.

"I think, actually, that it's blood."

She thought back to the night before, closed her eyes to remember the dark, imagined herself back on the ladder in the tunnel, listening. Without thinking why, she raised a hand to her cheek.

"Oh!" she said again.

Then, without another word, she ran out the door.

"I just remembered." Daphne was hurrying along the corridor, with Emily Lime and George trailing in her wake. "I'd forgotten. But I just remembered." Her voice was distant and distracted.

"Remembered what?" said George. "Where are we going?"

"I was hiding in the tunnel, and Cynthia had gone by. Then there was someone else. Two people, I think. I heard . . . some kind of argument. They were right above the trapdoor. I couldn't tell who it was, or what they said . . ."

She cast her mind back, remembering herself in the tunnel.

"They were whispering, of course."

"Then what?" said Emily Lime.

"Oh. Well, er . . . then I fell off the ladder."

Emily Lime rolled her eyes. "Fat lot of use you're going to be in the library if you fall off ladders. An assistant assistant librarian—"

"Well, I only fell off because"—Daphne came to a halt and touched a fingertip to her cheek again—"something dripped onto my face, in the dark, and, well, it gave me a bit of a shock and made me jump, so . . . I fell off. There was still something on my face this morning. Erica thought it was jam. But it can't have been. So I . . . I think it must have been blood."

George raised an eyebrow. Emily Lime looked skeptical.

Daphne checked each way along the corridor to make sure no one was coming, then she pointed at the rug by her feet.

"This is where the tunnel to the larder is. If it *was* blood on my face and dressing gown, it must have dripped through the knothole." Daphne crouched down and took hold of the rug. "So if Mr. Thanet didn't move the rug when he cleaned this morning, then there'll still be . . ."

She stood, lifting the rug to reveal the floor beneath.

It was spotless.

"Oh," said Daphne, disappointed. Then she saw how wide George's eyes were.

"Look," he said.

Daphne was still holding up the rug; George was pointing at the underside of it. There were two round dark-red stains.

"Looks like Thanet must have cleaned under the rug this morning, but not before some of the blood had soaked into it."

"So what?" said Emily Lime.

"What do you mean 'So what?'" said Daphne. "There was—"

"'Ey up!" George gave Daphne a nudge. "Bandits at three o'clock." He tilted his head to indicate a pair of teachers approaching from the far end of the corridor. Daphne swiftly replaced the rug, and the three of them set off back toward the library, mustering their most innocent faces for the teachers as they passed.

"There was blood on the floor!" said Daphne, once they were out of earshot.

"That's hardly unusual here," said Emily Lime. "I bet Thanet cleans some up most mornings. It's nothing to make a fuss about."

"Easy for you to say; you didn't have it pouring all over you."

They were at the steps that led to the library now. Emily Lime led them up and opened the door.

"Oh, don't be ridiculous," she said. "It was hardly pouring, was it? Barely a dribble by the sound of it."

They proceeded down into the body of the library.

"The important thing is we have the book back—even if we don't have its cover." She gave Daphne a dark look. "What we need to do now is get the lock fixed, then get back to business as usual. We've plenty to do. We need—"

"Bugs!" The Roar barged in through the door with all the grace and elegance of a battering ram. "What have you done with my flashlight?"

She stomped down the stairs and advanced toward them, her glowering expression exaggerated by her black eye.

"Your flashlight?" said George.

149

"Yes, my flashlight! I must have dropped it last night when I fell. Thanet says he didn't see it anywhere when he found me this morning, and it's not in the corridor now, so I assume one of you weeds must have nabbed it. So come on. Hand it over."

"We haven't got your stupid flashlight, Cynthia." George squared up to the head girl, looking her straight in the chin. "And don't you know this is a library? I know reading's a bit of a mystery to you but all the same, you should still know you're meant to be—"

"Quiet!" said Emily Lime, raising a thoughtful finger. She turned to the head girl. "Cynthia, was your flashlight on or off when you fell?"

"It was . . . oh, wait . . ." The Roar's sneering tone faded away as she struggled to remember. "I'd just turned it on when the door opened. I was going to shine it in the face of whoever was coming out. Blind them for a second. I'd just flicked the switch and then . . ." Her face fell. "And then I don't know what."

"But they didn't shine their flashlight at you?"

"Oh. No." The furrows in Cynthia's brow huddled together in deeper thought. "No, it was pitch-dark. They didn't have a flashlight at all, I don't think. That's odd, isn't it?"

"Yes, it is odd. But, of course, it does explain why *your* flashlight disappeared."

"How does it?" said Cynthia.

"Well," said Emily Lime wearily, "if whoever knocked you down the steps didn't have a flashlight, and they saw your flashlight lying there on the floor, shining in the darkness, then *obviously* they would have taken it to help them get away."

"Oh yes," said Cynthia. "That makes sense. So who-ever's got it now, they're to blame for this." She pointed with her good hand at her bad eye. "Well, they'll be in for it when I find them."

She headed back toward the door but turned to them before she left. "Oh, talking of finding people, have any of you squirts seen Veronica Keogh this morning?"

Daphne felt her whole body tighten. "Er, no. Why do you ask?"

"Silly little boil's gone missing. Probably just played hooky, but Bagley's making a fuss and talking about calling the police if she doesn't turn up soon. McKay's in a stinking mood about it." Cynthia pulled the door open. "If she turns up, send her to me so I can give her a piece of my mind."

"Are you sure you can spare it?" said George as the door squeaked closed behind her.

"Right, come on, then!" said Emily Lime. "Lots to do!"

Daphne, feeling a little dizzy, sank into a chair.

"How have we got lots to do?" said George.

"Financial planning," said Emily Lime. "We need to raise funds to pay for the books I ordered last week."

George looked furious. "You have to stop doing this! I keep telling you: *First* we get some money, *then* we order books. Not the other way round."

"But then we'd have to wait," said Emily Lime. "And anyway, we'll get the money."

"And how exactly are we going to do that?"

"Oh, you'll think of something."

"What about Veronica?" said Daphne.

"Oh," said Emily Lime. "Good point. Has she got money? Are her parents rich?"

"No," said Daphne, "I mean—"

"Orphan, I think," said George. "Parents died in the Blitz. She got shipped off to some rotten uncle in

Pilkington, but there was money in the will to pay her school fees. I assume her mum and dad thought she'd go somewhere decent, but the uncle sent her here instead. Paid the cheaper fees and pocketed the difference."

"No!" said Daphne insistently. "I mean, Veronica seems to be missing."

"Well? What if she is?" said Emily Lime.

"Aren't you concerned?"

Emily Lime and George looked at each other.

"I'm not concerned," said Emily Lime. "Are you concerned?"

"Not especially," said George.

"Oh, you're unbelievable!" said Daphne. "Both of you."

"Thank you very much," said George.

Then he took in the full extent of the unimpressed scowl that Daphne was firing his way. "Look, Daffers, I really don't think you need to worry about Veronica. Chances are she'll turn up soon enough. And besides, what do you want to do? Go to Mrs. McKay and tell her you heard . . . something, maybe,

while you were hiding in a secret tunnel on a jam-stealing raid?"

"Oh. I hadn't thought of that."

"No," said Emily Lime. "It seems to me you're not thinking very well at all. Far below the standards expected of an assistant assistant librarian. It's most disappointing." She scratched at her chin in a thoughtful manner. "But luckily I know a cure for that."

FIFTEEN

For reasons that Daphne didn't even slightly understand, she, George, and Emily Lime, all dressed in PE uniforms, were running across the sports field.

"Tell me ... again why ... we're ... doing this?" panted Daphne.

George, red-faced and breathless, took a moment to compose his reply.

"Bec-huff ... becooh-hfft ... because ..."

Then, having gotten one whole word out, he gave up and concentrated on not fainting from overexertion.

Even by his own low standards, George looked

terrible. His shorts were ragged and crumpled, his shirt was muddy and shapeless, and his socks appeared to have a fear of heights. The entire outfit gave off a musty scent, as if, perhaps, his clothing had remained unworn and unwashed in a drawer for months, slowly festering. Which of course it had.

Daphne, in contrast, was well turned out in crisp, clean, fragrant clothes, but was almost as unable as George to cope with the unfamiliar physical exertion of a cross-country run.

They crossed the playing fields and cut through a corner of the woods, then made their way down the side of a plowed field.

"I mean . . ." she puffed, ". . . she's a . . . librarian. Surely . . . she ought to be . . . an indoors type." Daphne gulped in a couple of lungfuls and waited for a dizzy spell to pass. "You know . . . bookish."

Emily Lime, too far ahead of them to hear any of this, trotted steadily on. There was nothing graceful about her, and she ran with an awkward stoop, but she kept up a good pace. Reaching the end of the field, she leapt with surprising ease across the ditch that marked its boundary and landed nimbly on the far side without breaking her stride.

George and Daphne, approaching the ditch with much less speed and confidence, slowed to a halt. Then, having silently agreed that jumping was not an option, they climbed awkwardly down the near bank.

"She's got this idea that running about like a loon helps you think," said George. "Something about increasing blood flow to the brain. She read it in a book, apparently. Like most of—oh, mind out, it's pretty muddy down here—like most of her daft ideas."

"And does it work?" Daphne tried to pick out a dry route to the other side.

"Oh, it works all right," said George. "It works just fine—*for her*. Otherwise, it depends on whether or not it kills you."

If there *was* a dry route across the bottom of the ditch, then it certainly wasn't the way that George had gone. He was ankle-deep in cloying mud and flapping his arms about as if trying to fly himself free.

"Mind you, if it did kill us, I s'pose that would seem an appropriate end now that we seem to be reenacting the First World War."

He lurched forward, his feet encased in gloop, onto the far bank.

"Lovely," he said, examining the damage.

Daphne spotted a relatively dry patch on the far side. If she could land there, she thought, she might just keep her gym shoes from being entirely ruined.

"Well, it's certainly got me thinking," she said as she

tensed herself ready to jump. "But mostly about inventive ways to murder assistant librarians."

It was not much of a jump, but exhaustion and irritation made it seem more of a challenge than it really was. Daphne rocked her weight back onto one foot, then forward again, and pushed off. Her other foot sailed confidently toward her target. Then it hit, and broke through the deceptive crust on the surface to thick ooze below. Her heel skidded forward, her weight was thrown backward, and down she went, flat on her back in the thick of it.

She raised her head, mud gluing her hair to the back of her head, rivulets of brownish water running down her face, and saw George wobbling above her looking concerned, and behind him, Emily Lime, a healthy rosy glow coloring her cheeks and a well-practiced frown occupying the rest of her face.

"Come *on*! We can't hang around playing in the mud, you know. We have things to do."

After some grumbling and a good deal of sliding about, George got Daphne onto her feet, and the pair of them climbed unsteadily out of the ditch to where Emily was standing, hands on hips, looking purposeful. They slumped at her.

"So," said Emily Lime, "what do we think?"

"Think?" said Daphne. "Well, I'll tell you what I think. I think that this is no way to treat a newly recruited assistant assistant librarian. I think I'm cold and dirty and wet and *outside*, and I don't want to be any of those things. I think you're probably mad. I think that if I don't die, then my parents will kill me for ruining my gym uniform. And—and—and . . ." She could hear how high-pitched her voice had become. "And you haven't even given me my badges yet!" she shrieked. Then she slumped forward, hugging her knees to her chest, and pouted in as childish a fashion as she could.

"Yes," said Emily, unmoved by Daphne's theatrics. "But never mind all that. How are we going to raise some cash to pay our book bill?"

"How can you even think about that?" said Daphne. "In fact, how can you think about anything? I'm too tired and miserable to think at all!"

But Daphne realized that that wasn't really true. The exercise and her anger had kick-started her brain into life. As soon as the break-in entered her head, her thoughts went racing.

"Although . . ." she said.

"What?" said Emily Lime.

"I've been thinking about flashlights."

"What about them?" said Emily Lime.

"Well, as you said, you don't come to a break-in equipped with a crowbar but forget to bring a flashlight."

"So?" said George.

"So they *did* have a flashlight when they went into the library."

"But . . . ?" said Emily Lime.

"But they didn't have one when they left."

"Eh?" said George. "But why—?"

"Because"—Daphne smiled—"you're meant to be quiet."

"What are you—"

"Come on," said Daphne, leaping to her feet. "We have to go back to the library." And with that, she leapt straight over the ditch and began to run back toward the school.

"Oh lumme!" said George, climbing down into the ditch again as Emily Lime sprang across the gap. "Hold up! Wait for me!"

SIXTEEN

Daphne left a trail of mud all along the corridor to the library door. By the time Emily Lime arrived, Daphne was already on her hands and knees down by the crime books. When George got in—radiating impressive heat from his purple face, his every breath creaking like a rusty gate—he took a quick look up at the Beast's basket, to make sure it wasn't occupied, then he, too, fell to his hands and knees, albeit for different reasons.

"What . . . ?" said George.

"Why are . . . ?" he continued.

"What . . . ?" he elaborated.

Then he moved himself into a sitting position, propped against the barren shelves of the drama section, and concentrated on not being sick. He watched the girls for a moment or two. Emily was emptying a wastepaper basket that was opposite the crime shelves, while Daphne was padding about like a police dog sniffing for clues.

"What... *are* you doing?" George said.

"Oh, well, I *thought* I had it all figured out," said Daphne, rising to her feet and adopting a hands-on-hips annoyed pose to match her voice. She stomped over to the crime shelves, once again playacting the part of the imagined intruder. She hunched a little, mimed holding a flashlight in one hand while the pointed finger of the other hand ran along the spines of the books.

"So, imagine I'm whoever it was who broke in. And I'm not here just to make a mess. I'm looking for a book. I'm looking for one particular book, but I can't find it."

"Yes?" said Emily Lime.

"And so I'm frustrated and annoyed, so I throw some books to the floor."

Daphne mimed pulling books from the shelf and casting them onto the floor.

"Oh, I see," said George. "And that's enough of a racket to attract the attention of the Roar."

"Yes. But before she gets here, I drop my flashlight. A flashlight that, if I'm a pupil here, has my name scratched on it."

"Right!" George caught on, at last. "So if we can find it, then we'll know who broke in. But why would you—I mean, why would they drop it?"

"Because when they made enough noise for Cynthia to hear—" said Daphne.

"They also woke up the Beast, in its basket on top of the bookshelf," said Emily Lime.

"And," said Daphne, "from what you've said, he doesn't like to be—oh, or is it she?"

"It's 'it,'" said Emily Lime.

"Right. Well, I'm guessing *it* doesn't like to be disturbed."

"Oh. I see," said George.

"And judging by the way its basket has shifted along the top of the shelves from where it was yesterday,

I would say it jumped out in this direction, to land on whoever had woken it up by throwing books about."

"Oh."

Daphne resumed her role.

"So, I'm annoyed that I can't find the book. I throw some of the other books to the floor—thump, thump, thump—the Beast wakes up, jumps on me"—Daphne staggered backward, one hand clawing at an imaginary horror in front of her face, her other arm thrown out and backward—"and I drop my flashlight"—she turned herself round while keeping her arm in place, pointing to the area she and Emily had just been searching— "there." A look of tight frustration took hold of her face. "But it's not there!"

George, who by now was only pink in the face and more or less able to breathe normally, took her place in front of the shelves and pondered for a moment.

"But what if they had the flashlight in the other hand . . . ?"

He did his own bit of playacting, staggering, hand to face, other hand thrust backward. He turned to find he was pointing at the shelves of the art section, which contained only a very worn copy of a book about nudes.

"Oh," he said. "It's not there either." His face deflated.

"No," said Emily Lime as she stomped over to take her turn in front of the bookcase. "But you're forgetting that the Roar said the intruder was tall. So this affects several of the variables in your simulation. So the flashlight begins higher up."

She raised a hand above her own head height.

"Then we adjust the trajectory to account for longer arms, giving more thrust . . ."

With none of the drama that Daphne and George had put into their reenactments, Emily Lime pointed her arm out, back, and up. Then she turned round with her arm held still, gazed along it, and extended her index finger.

"Artists *A* to *Z*," she said. "Top shelf, *A* to *D*. Right-hand side. Just about where Dürer will go."

They all looked up at the shelf, which was way above their eyeline. If there was anything there, then it was hidden from their view.

Emily Lime turned to George. "Get the steps."

George whizzed off and soon returned with the library's set of wooden steps on wheels. He positioned them by the art section and climbed up. Even on the top step, he still could not see into the top shelf and had to reach up and fumble with a searching hand in the spot Emily Lime had indicated.

"Well?" said Daphne.
George began to giggle.

Then he turned and, with a dramatic flourish, held up a rather battered-looking flashlight.

"Ta-da!"

Daphne gasped.

Emily Lime gave a tiny nod of satisfaction.

George flashed the flashlight on and off and danced a celebratory jig at the top of the steps.

"Haroo!" he yelled, grinning like a lunatic.

"And is there a name on it?" said Daphne.

"Well, Daffers," said George, still dancing, "let's just take a look, shall we?" He raised the flashlight up in front of his face to give it his full attention.

Then he fell off backward.

SEVENTEEN

George's cheek hurt. Why was that? Had he landed on it when he fell? Surely the rest of his face ought to hurt, too, if that was it. But it didn't. He had a few minor pains in his chest and arms, but they were quite dull aches, whereas the pain in his cheek was much more intense. It *stung*, that was the word, almost as if someone had—

Matron slapped him again, even harder than the first time, and George's eyes snapped open.

"Ah!"

There were two main reasons why the students of

St. Rita's, no matter how sick they got, avoided visiting the sanatorium. The first was the wallpaper, which was a peculiarly stomach-churning shade of yellow. The second and more significant reason was Matron, who possessed no shred of medical knowledge, training, or indeed sympathy, compassion, or humanity. One of the less fanciful rumors about Matron was that she had only come to St. Rita's after her international wrestling career had come to a controversial end following the death of (depending on which version of the story you heard) an opponent, a referee, or both. Certainly the force of her slap gave George no reason to disbelieve any of these theories.

"Feeling much better now. Thanks so much," he said, and gave his jaw a wiggle just to check it was still properly attached.

"See?" said Matron to Emily Lime. "I told you he'd be fine. I am proper good at my job, you know. When I make someone well, they stay well. Do you know, I don't think I've ever treated the same girl twice."

She held up a hand the size of a small gravestone for their inspection. "I suppose I must have healing hands."

"Extraordinary," said Emily Lime, which it certainly was.

George sat up on the narrow sanatorium bed, gave his cheek a rub, and swung his legs round to lower himself to the floor.

"Right. We'll be off, then, Matron."

"No. You have to stay."

"No, really. I'm feeling absolutely fine now. You've worked wonders. It's amazing, really, considering how far I fell."

Having said this, he realized it was true. He'd only said it to get away as quickly as possible, but actually, it really *was* amazing that he didn't feel worse.

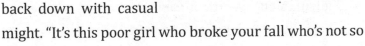

"Of course *you're* fine," said Matron, placing a hand on George's shoulder and pressing him back down with casual might. "It's this poor girl who broke your fall who's not so fine."

She pointed a sausage-like finger at the other bed, where Daphne lay inert.

171

"So, you'll be a gent and wait for her, now, won't you?"

"Daphne!" George dropped down to the floor and took two quick paces over to Daphne's bed.

"She's unconscious," said Matron. "But don't worry, I'll soon . . ." She paced over toward Daphne, raising a slab-like hand above her head as she went.

"No!" said George, doing his best to block Matron's path. "Um, do you have any smelling salts, maybe?" he said. "Only, Daphne's, er . . . Daphne's got, er . . . she's got quite flaky skin, actually. Some kind of rash. It's not too bad at the moment—you'd barely notice it—but I think she said it's contagious. So, might be best if you . . . you know . . . don't touch?"

Matron considered this. A look of sour distaste on her face gave way to one of bitter disappointment.

"Well," she said, "I don't like to—I don't hold with these newfangled scientific ways . . . I prefer to rely on my natural healing gifts . . . but under the circumstances, I suppose I could give it a try. Hang on."

She rumbled over to a cabinet marked with a red cross that was mounted to the wall, unlocked it, and examined the jumbled contents. After a good deal of picking up and putting down various bottles and jars, Matron eventually selected a small brown glass bottle

half-full of a clear liquid. She wiped a layer of grime off the label and held it very close to her eyes, her lips moving as she read.

"Well, it's a bit out of date, but it's probably fine," she said, and unscrewed the lid.

She pushed past George and held the open bottle under Daphne's nose, wafting it from side to side as a pale green thread of vapor rose from its mouth. George watched as Daphne's nostrils twitched once, then twice more, then flared wide open as her eyelids peeled back to reveal eyes bulging so much that they looked like they were trying to break free. Daphne sat bolt upright as tears trailed down her cheeks and her mouth stretched wide to release a bellow of anguished distress.

"NNYEEEEEUUUUUURRRRRRRGH!"

Then she fell silent, her streaming eyes locked open, her mouth gaping wordlessly, her body rocking gently with her breathing.

"Well," said Matron at last, "that seems to have done the trick." She replaced the lid, with newfound respect, and returned the bottle to the medicine cabinet.

"Are you all right?" said George.

"It buuuurns!" croaked Daphne.

Between the two beds, on a small table, was a glass vase full of long-dead flowers. Daphne grabbed it, yanked out the dried-out stems, and gulped down the murky green water that remained. Her face distorted in disgust.

"Better?" said George, stooping to pick up the discarded flowers.

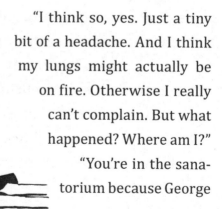

"I think so, yes. Just a tiny bit of a headache. And I think my lungs might actually be on fire. Otherwise I really can't complain. But what happened? Where am I?"

"You're in the sana-torium because George

was an idiot and fell on you and knocked you out," said Emily Lime.

"Sorry about that," said George.

"That's okay," said Daphne, wincing slightly as she swung herself out of the bed. "I think I was sort of trying to catch you, actually, so I brought it on myself. But can we move quickly away from this wallpaper now? Otherwise I think my headache's just going to get worse."

"Yuss, let's," said George. "Thanks so much, Matron. We'll be off now. You put your feet up and have a rest. Been a busy day for you already, hasn't it?"

"Ooh, yes. You pair and before that the Rawlinson girl, too. What was she thinking needing medical attention that early in the morning, anyway? Uncivilized, I call it. And then she was ranting and raving when she was here, blabbering all kinds of nonsense, until I knocked some sense into her. Not that she was grateful."

Matron lowered her voice to a whisper, leaning in to the children as they made their way to the door. "She used language! I've a good mind to tell the head."

"Well, yes, you should probably do exactly that," said George, opening the door.

"She was swearing at me, bold as brass, as she left. Disgraceful, it was."

"Appalling," agreed George as he made his way out with Emily Lime and Daphne close behind.

"Made me clean forget to give her back her note."

The six-legged George/Emily/Daphne procession came to a halt.

"Note?" said George.

"What note would that be?" said Daphne.

Matron fished a crumpled scrap from her pocket.

"Fell out of her pocket when Thanet laid her out on the bed."

"Would you like us to get it back to her, Matron?" said George. "Save you the bother? You deserve a rest after all your hard work this morning."

"Oh, well, if you don't mind."

"Not at all," said George, plucking the scrap of paper from Matron's giant hand. "We'd be delighted."

EIGHTEEN

W hat does it say?"

They were marching along the corridor toward the library. George uncrumpled the paper and examined it.

"It's a tip-off! *Larder raid. 10:45 tonight!*"

"Veronica," said Daphne.

"Dunno," said George. "It's not signed."

"It had to be Veronica. The raid was going to be at midnight until she said to make it earlier. She chose the time. But she said 10:30, not 10:45."

"But why ...?"

"I have no idea."

"I think you're both forgetting about this," said Emily Lime, holding up a flashlight.

"I was just coming to that," lied George.

Emily Lime handed him the flashlight.

"Here you are, then. What does it tell you?"

George turned it in his hands, examining it closely from all angles while making occasional contemplative humming noises.

"Well?" said Emily Lime.

"It's a flashlight," said George.

"And?" said Emily Lime.

"It's a bit dented?"

"You dropped it from the top of the steps onto the library floor."

"Ah," said George.

"Shortly after you'd mauled any fingerprints—if it ever came to that—that might have been on it with those filthy fingers of yours."

"Oops," said George. "So it doesn't tell us anything!"

"Well, maybe it does," said Daphne. "I think all the girls on the raid last night had a flashlight, and they were all the same kind."

"Yes. We all get them at the shop in Pelham," said George.

"But this one's different, which I think means the intruder must have come from outside the school. And—"

"What ho, bookworms!"

Marion parked herself beside the steps to the library as Daphne, George, and Emily Lime arrived. "Oh, I say, this is a stroke of luck. I was just looking for you lot. Is this one of yours?"

She thrust a hand out in front of her, clutching a rather mangled, but familiar, book.

"In a bit of a state, I'm afraid. Like that when I got it, though. Found it out on the playing field, having a stroll with Cicely after breakfast. It's a rum one, though. You'd think from that cover it'd be a hot bit of stuff, but it's a real letdown: It's actually the most awful tosh about some wet girl and her soppy kitten. Still, any use to you?"

Emily Lime, tight-faced and silent, took it from her with a curt nod.

"You're very welcome," said Marion. "Oh, I say, you haven't seen Keyhole, have you?"

"Veronica?" said Daphne. "No. So she's still missing?"

"Apparently. Hulky's been looking for her all morning and—"

"Hulky?"

"Seraphina Holcroft. Big gorilla of a girl. King Kong in a pinafore, but not so dainty."

"Oh yes," said Daphne, remembering the girl she had seen with Veronica outside the dorm.

"Anyway, Hulky's the sort who, if she's asking you a question, you give her a straight answer—but she's asked half the school and apparently nobody's seen Ronnie since last night. Seems Ronnie owes Hulky for some bit of business she did for her yesterday. Bagley wants to call the cops and report her as a missing person. McKay's dead set against it, as per. Says she'll turn up eventually. Rather hope she doesn't, to be honest, considering everything that Hulky says she wants to do to her for welshing on their deal. You know, I wouldn't have had her down as a scholar at all, but old Hulky's knowledge of anatomy is really rather impressive. She knew the Latin names for all the parts she said she'd break. Anyway, if you do spot Keyhole, then tell her to lie low for . . . oh, I don't know . . . a decade or so, until Hulky's calmed down. Oh, and tell her I've put her blessed kangaroo back in her bed."

"RooRoo?" said Daphne.

"I beg your pardon, old girl. Are you quite all right?"

"Oh. Yes. But what was that about Veronica's kangaroo?"

"Oh, well, funny business, that. That was out on the field, too. Gone for a hop, I suppose. Found it out there after we found the book. Quite the lost property jamboree!"

Daphne felt a knot in her stomach tighten. Surely

Veronica wouldn't leave the school without taking her precious kangaroo with her.

"Anyway, what are you bookworms dressed like this for?" Marion wafted a hand in the direction of George's clothing, while being careful to keep a safe distance. "Holding your own sports day or something? You know the big lacrosse game isn't till tomorrow?"

"Eh? Oh, right," said George, looking down at his mud-spattered PE uniform.

Marion eyed him with a pitying expression.

"You know, I could put you in touch with a very good tailor, if you liked. Chap I use in Pilkington. Absolute genius. He could make you look . . . well, a bit less awful, at any rate."

"Thanks a bunch," said George.

"Oh, no trouble," said Marion cheerily. "I could put a word in next Tuesday. Got to nip into town to meet some fellow at the bank and get a new account opened. That's the problem with having money, I suppose. Frightful nuisance working out what to do with it all."

"Sounds awful," said Daphne.

"Oh, well, I dare say I'll get through somehow," said Marion. "Cheerio."

"Bloomin' cheek," said George as she marched away.

NINETEEN

Inside the library, Emily Lime, George, and Daphne gathered round the table where Emily Lime had placed the copy of *Scarlet Fury* next to the damaged copy of *Daisy's Little Kitten*. Her hands were shaking as she swapped the dust jackets back, and her breathing was unusually loud.

"Just look at this!" she said in a cracked voice, holding up *Daisy's Little Kitten* in delicate hands. The cover was only barely attached at the top of the spine, as if someone had tried to tear it off entirely. "What kind of *monster* could do such a thing?"

"A discerning critic of literary fiction?" said George. "Or someone who hates kittens?"

"Or books," said Daphne.

"Hates books?" Emily Lime's face shriveled at the very idea. "How could anyone—?"

"And of course Cynthia was quite badly hurt," said Daphne, who thought that one less copy of *Daisy's Little Kitten* in the world could only be a good thing.

"*She'll* mend," said Emily Lime. "But this . . . The barbarity!"

She laid the book back down on the table.

"I'll fetch the glue," said George, slapping a consoling hand on Emily Lime's shoulder as he passed.

"You know," said Daphne, "if Veronica was trying to steal *this*"—she tapped a finger on *Scarlet Fury*—"then maybe whoever broke into the library was after it, too."

"I don't see why," said Emily Lime.

George returned to the table with an old newspaper, a pot of paste, and a brush.

"No," he said, laying out the newspaper. "I mean it's a good 'un, but you wouldn't break down a door for it."

He placed *Daisy's Little Kitten* on the newspaper and hummed to himself as, with a few neat movements, he glued the cover back into place.

"Here, Daffers"—he handed the book to Daphne—"put some pressure on there, will you? Just until the glue's dried."

Daphne pressed her palm against the spine of the book.

George assessed it with a glance, and gave a satisfied nod.

"Now, what can we do about you?" He picked up *Scarlet Fury*, brushed a clod of dirt from its jacket, and ran his finger along a jagged tear. "That bloomin' kitten stole your coat and didn't look after it, did it?" he said, in a singsong voice. He gave the book a pat and turned it over in his hands. "But a bit of sticky tape will stop that tear from getting any worse."

George started to flick through the pages from the back. "And at least your insides are all fine and—oh! What's this?"

The book fell open at a spot near the back where, tucked between the pages, there was a folded sheet of newspaper. George plucked it out and began to unfold it.

"It's a crossword," he said. "Not many of the answers are filled in, though. Reckon Mrs. Crump must have used it as a bookmark."

"What else is on there?" said Daphne.

George passed the paper to her. "See for yourself."

Daphne unfolded the paper twice more, doubling and redoubling the size, revealing a full page of the *Pilkington Chronicle*, very slightly yellowed with age.

"Crikey!" said Daphne, seeing the headline. *"Criminal Mastermind Sought by Police After Daring Bank Raid."* She read on. *"Police were called this morning to the Pilkington District Bank following a daring raid on their high-security vault*—blah, blah—*fifty deposit boxes broken into . . . jewelry stolen*—blah, blah, blah—*value in excess of one hundred thousand pounds . . . !"*

"Oh yes!" said George. "I heard about this. This was weeks ago, wasn't it?"

Daphne checked the date on the page. "Yes, er . . . just over three months ago, in fact."

She returned to the article.

"Police are seeking the bank's cleaner, Mr. Frederick Barnum . . . known to the police, following a string of convictions for burglary in the late forties . . . set up a cleaning business two years ago . . . the bank took him on six months ago. Inspector Bright of the Pilkington constabulary told the Chronicle: *'We believe this robbery to be the work of a single perpetrator, though we cannot speculate at this time as to that individual's identity.' However, sources*

close to the inspector later confirmed that Fred Barnum—
aka Lampshade Fred—was 'a right iffy character and no
mistake' and that finding him was a high priority in the
investigation . . . Then there's a telephone number to call
for anyone with *information pertaining to the crime.*"

Daphne set the paper down on the table for the
others to examine.

"And look, someone has underlined the bit about
how much the robbers got away with, and put two
exclamation marks after it. And the name of the police
inspector and the telephone number are both circled."

"That's not Mrs. Crump, then," said George. "She can't
abide exclamation marks. And three months ago is
before we got given the Smeeton Westerby books, isn't
it?" He looked to Emily Lime.

"Yes. A little before."

"So the newspaper could already have been inside the book when it was donated."

"Who did donate the books?" said Daphne.

"Somebody's aunt, I think," said George. "Do you remember, Lime?"

"Mrs. Crump dealt with it. There might be a record of it somewhere. I'll look."

Emily Lime headed for her office.

"So," said Daphne, "the school was broken into—"

"Well, we don't know that," said George.

"Don't we? Do any of the girls have a flashlight like the one you found? And remember, the window to the chemistry lab was open all night, so if there was an intruder, they could easily have gotten in without leaving a trace. Especially if they were an experienced burglar like—"

"Lampshade Fred!" said George. "It could have been him!"

"Must have been!" said Daphne.

"Nonsense!" said Emily Lime, shouting from the office. "If that newspaper article is three months old, then surely even this dim Inspector Bright must have caught him by now."

George looked crestfallen, but Daphne didn't.

"Actually, no," she said. "There was a newspaper left

on the train yesterday, and I was so bored I read most of it. It had a follow-up article about the robbery: *Criminal Mastermind Still at Large*. It said the police are no closer to solving the case. Lampshade Fred's still loose, and the loot's still missing."

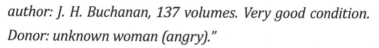

"Mrs. Crump's filing methods really are infuriatingly unprofessional," said Emily Lime, returning to the table with a scrap of paper in her hand. "Just look at this." She held the scrap up in front of her face. *"Smeeton Westerby crime novels, author: J. H. Buchanan, 137 volumes. Very good condition. Donor: unknown woman (angry)."*

"Oh," said George. "Come to think of it, I do remember Mrs. C mentioning an angry woman. Apparently the books were her husband's. They'd had a bust-up, so she donated his books to spite him."

"Interesting," said Daphne. "So maybe the husband broke into the library to try to get the book back."

"Highly unlikely," said Emily Lime.

"Well, yes," said Daphne. "But it looks as if Veronica wanted it, and someone else went to the bother of breaking in, so there must be something about it to make it worth the trouble. And if it's connected to this bank robbery in some weird way . . . Well then, a hundred thousand pounds' worth of jewelry would seem like a pretty good incentive, don't you think?"

"That's ridiculous—" said Emily Lime.

"Oh, and did I say that the article mentioned a reward for any information leading to the recovery of the jewels?"

"Ooh," said George. "Enough to buy some books?"

"Hundreds," said Daphne.

"As I was saying," said Emily Lime, "that's ridiculously convincing, and we must investigate."

"Great," said Daphne. "But how?"

George sprang to his feet. Even in the short time she had known him, Daphne had come to realize that springing was not something George did often, so it seemed significant.

"Come on," he said. "It's high time we changed out of our gym uniforms."

Daphne was disappointed. She had been sure he was about to say something surprising or dramatic, and that really didn't fit the bill.

"And then," said George, "we need to go and talk to a nun about a bank robbery."

TWENTY

F red Barnum, you say?"

Sister Adelaide inhaled the last gasp of her current cigarette, stubbed out the end in a grubby saucer already brimming with butts and ash, and rummaged in her desk drawer looking for a successor.

"Whaddya wanna know?"

"We were wondering if you'd heard anything about this?" said George, holding up the newspaper clipping.

"Oh yes?" said Sister Adelaide, barely glancing at the paper, and pushing the drawer as closed as its overflowing contents would allow. "And why you askin'?"

She moved her search to the desktop, lifting and shifting papers, books, and filthy teacups at random.

As the fug of cigarette smoke that filled the small room dissipated slightly, Daphne was able to get a clearer view of this odd little woman. Her sharp eyes danced as her fingers, stained as yellow as the peeling wallpaper, scrabbled through the detritus on the desktop, and her pinched lips twitched and pursed beneath her eagle's beak of a nose.

"Apparently there's a reward for information leading to his arrest, so if you knew anything, then—"

"Hah!" Sister Adelaide straightened in her chair, one triumphant hand clutching a crumpled cigarette packet. "Well, if I knew anything about that, then I'd just tell the coppers meself, wouldn't I, Georgie boy."

She rummaged in the packet and extracted the one remaining cigarette, then set about trying to straighten it.

"But old Fred never done that bank job. He's been framed. He ain't no bank robber. He wasn't even a good burglar—he'd be even worse as a bank robber. See what it says there?"

Satisfied with her repairs, she planted the cigarette into one side of her mouth, then continued to speak through the other side. "*Mr. Barnum is well-known to the* police, *following a string of convictions for burglary.* That's not a criminal mastermind, is it? Yer criminal mastermind don't get caught once, let alone a string of times. Yer criminal mastermind don't even do no crimes himself. He just plans 'em and gets some other mug to do the dirty work. Nah, yer proper criminal master-mind, yer don't even know his name. Yer don't even know he exists."

She struck a match, put the flame to the tip of her cigarette, and sucked meanly at it. "If Lampshade Fred is a criminal mastermind, then I'm the bloomin' pope."

She took another hefty drag on her cigarette, then lifted it from her lips, gesturing to emphasize her point. "And I ain't."

Half an inch of ash dropped down her front.

"Fact is, what I heard was, he really had gone straight. But I don't hold that against him, mind. Decent fella at heart, old Lampshade. Just not really cut out for a life of crime."

"You can't be *sure* it wasn't him, though," said Daphne.

Sister Adelaide cocked an eyebrow at her and gave Daphne a stare so hard that it easily penetrated the wall of smoke between them.

"I can be, and I am, missy. See, I know criminal types. And, of course, you can't trust 'em. That's the point. But with Lampshade, his problem was not just the burglaries he done—though Gawd knows they was bad enough—but even when he didn't get caught straight off, he'd be so pleased with himself he'd go blurtin' about the job to some bloke in a pub—boastin' like—and then some blighter'd turn him in."

"But—"

"And even if he didn't do *that*, he'd get caught tryin' to sell his loot. He's such an unlucky mug that the usual fences—that's the fellas what sell on yer stolen goods, missy—won't do business with him, see? So he'd try to do it hisself. Once he tried to sell a solid gold tie pin to a bloke in a pub; turned out it was the bloomin' chief inspector of police. Now, whoever's done this bank job, on the other hand, I reckon they've been right smart about it. I would've heard if all them sparklers had been sold on, see; but I ain't, so they ain't. So what I reckon is: Whoever's got 'em is playin' it cool. They've got 'em hidden somewhere safe and they're just gonna leave 'em there until everything's cooled down. Now *that's* more like yer criminal mastermind. Cool and patient, like. And, you know, not—with all due respect to Lampshade—an idiot."

Sister Adelaide paused a moment, sucked the last bit of life out of her ciggy, and then ground the stub out in her ashtray saucer.

"So that's what I know, young George."

Sister Adelaide blew out a blast of air, poking a hole in the cloud of smoke in front of her face through which her beady stare bore into George's eyes. "So what do *you* know? You ain't askin' for the good of your health."

"Oh, we just thought, you know, there's a burglar on the loose, and somebody broke into the library . . ."

"But I thought that was meant to be one of the girls. An' I thought nothing went missing? What ain't you tellin' me, Georgie?"

"Oh, er, well . . ."

"We thought all the girls here would know there's nothing worth breaking into the library for," said Daphne. "Only an outsider could think it was worth the trouble."

"Huh. Makes sense, I s'pose," huffed Sister Adelaide. "But I don't reckon it's Lampshade. I mean, it sounds like a right botch job, so that much fits. But he ain't much of a reader, I don't reckon, so he'd hardly be likely to rob a library. And with the police so keen to have a chat with him, I reckon even old Fred would have the sense to clear off out of town. Got family up in Scotland, I heard. Probably lyin' low in the highlands, I reckon. That all, is it?"

George and Daphne looked glum.

"Yes, that was all," said George.

"Then you've been keepin' me from my holy contemplations long enough," said Sister Adelaide, raising a copy of the *Racing Post* from her desk and turning her attention to the runners and riders in the 3:30 at Chepstow.

"Righto, Sister," said George, taking a fresh packet of cigarettes from his blazer pocket and tossing it onto the desk. "Thanks for your time, anyway."

"Obliged to you, Georgie boy." Sister Adelaide gave a thankful nod as she opened the packet.

Outside in the corridor, Daphne took in a deep breath.

"At last," she said. "Fresh air! Those cigarettes were vile!"

"French," said George.

"And did you see," said Daphne, "she had ash all down her clothes?"

"Yes," said Emily Lime. "It's a filthy habit."

"And does she actually *teach* here?"

"Divinity and philosophy. Oh, and she runs the martial arts club after lessons on Tuesdays, if you're interested. But I wouldn't advise it."

"And is she really a nun?"

"Oh yes," said George. "Before she came to teaching she used to be in a mission in London, working in the roughest areas, trying to reform criminal types."

"I see. And that's how she knows so much about them?"

"Kind of. I think in the end it was more that they reformed her in the opposite direction. But either way, she knows a handy amount about the criminal underworld."

"Of course," said Emily Lime, "logically, if the bank robber wasn't this Lightbulb Jim—"

"Lampshade Fred," corrected George.

"And our intruder wasn't him either, then it is possible . . ."

"Oh!" said Daphne. "I see."

"What do you see?" said George.

"Whoever robbed the bank could still be our burglar."

"Oh."

"And if so . . ." said Daphne, "and if, for whatever reason, they really want the book . . ."

George's eyes bulged wide open.

"Then they'll come back!"

TWENTY-ONE

"We have to tell Mrs. McKay," said Daphne.

"Fat lot of good that'll do us," said George, shambling after her in the direction of the head's office. Emily Lime had gone to see Mr. Thanet about getting a new lock fitted to the library door.

"But someone broke into the school, and Veronica has gone missing, and it's probably her blood we saw . . . Surely she has to do *something*."

"Well, you would think so. But I doubt it. If it was a member of Mrs. McKay's precious lacrosse team who'd gone missing, then maybe she'd care. But Ronnie? Never in a million years."

"But you said yourself: Whoever broke in will probably come back to try again."

"Oh yes, that's what *I* think. But you'd never convince Mrs. McKay."

"Well . . . I have to at least try."

They had arrived outside Mrs. McKay's office. Daphne stood before the door, settled herself, stood up straight, and as she rehearsed in her head what she wanted to say, she raised her fist and knocked.

The door must not have been closed properly, and it swung open to reveal that Mrs. McKay wasn't even

there—but there *was* a girl. She was older than Daphne, and she had a sheaf of paperwork in her hand and a single sheet clamped between her lips. She looked startled when the door opened, but at the sight of George, relief washed over her face. She took the sheet of paper from her mouth and placed it on top of the filing cabinet where she was standing.

"Blimey, George!" she said, turning her attention back to the contents of the top drawer. "You scared the life out of me! I thought Mrs. Mac was back early. Who's your pal?"

"Oh, hello, Peters," said George. "This is Daphne Blakeway. Daphne, this is Peters. Daphne wanted to see Mrs. McKay, but as she's not here, we'll push—"

"Oh," said Daphne. "Peters! Marion mentioned you. She said you're a whiz at picking locks. Is that how you let yourself in? How fabulous!"

Daphne flashed a quick look each way along the corridor, then stepped into the office herself. "Can you really do it with a hairpin like in the movies?"

"Nah!" Peters scowled. "You don't want to believe everything you see at the pictures, you know."

Daphne looked deflated.

"You need *two* hairpins."

Daphne wandered over to the desk. Peters cast her a wary glance.

"Don't get comfortable; she'll be back in a bit—I seen her diary. She's got an appointment in a few minutes. Ronnie Keogh's uncle."

"Oh yes. He must be worried."

"Well, if he didn't want to be worried, then he shouldn't have sent her here, should he?" Peters pulled a fistful of paperwork from the drawer.

"What are you doing?" said Daphne.

"McKay keeps files about all the girls. There's a girl in the upper sixth needs hers changing. Her parents said they'd take her out of school if her behavior didn't improve. So I'm improving her behavior. Editing out some of the detentions, the late homework, the criminal charges, that sort of thing. Ah! Here we are."

Peters dumped the bundle of papers she was holding onto the desk while giving her full attention to the sheet she had just plucked from the cabinet. After a brief read, she screwed it up and stuffed it in her pocket, then took the sheet from the top of the cabinet and placed it in the drawer.

Daphne glanced at the paperwork on top of the desk.

"Make yourself useful and pass us that lot, will you?"

said Peters. "I need to get this place looking how I found it sharpish."

Daphne picked up a bundle in each hand and passed the first one to Peters.

"Hear that, George? She's back any minute, so we can see her after all."

"Bloomin' marvelous," said George, nervously staring off down the corridor again.

Daphne passed Peters the second bundle, picked up the remaining pile of papers from the desktop, and glanced at the top sheet.

"Oh!" Daphne's eyes raced across the page. "Oh!"

"Never mind reading it!" Peters held her hand out. "Hand it over!"

When Daphne made no move to do as she was told, Peters snatched the papers from her, dropped them into the filing cabinet, and closed the drawer.

"Out! Now!"

Daphne sleepwalked obediently out of the office past a bemused George while Peters locked the filing cabinet, despite not having a key.

"What is it?" said George.

Daphne just stared at him.

"You know, George," said Peters as she emerged from the office and closed the door, "I don't mind an audience, but your pal here is a liability."

She crouched by the keyhole, inserted two bent pieces of wire, and fiddled with them for a second. There was a click as the door locked.

Peters stood up. "I don't appreciate it." She gave Daphne a scowl, then set off quickly and silently away from them just as footsteps began to sound distantly from the other direction.

"Well, I suppose that'll be Mrs. Mac coming back." George stared toward the sound. "If you really want to—"

"No!" Daphne said. "No. Let's go." She tugged at George's sleeve.

"Well, make your bloomin' mind up. For heaven's—" George saw the urgent look in Daphne's eyes. "Righto."

They hurried away after Peters.

Round the corner and safely out of sight, George pulled Daphne to a halt by her shirtsleeve.

"Well, what was that all about?"

"There was a letter from the bank," said Daphne. "In the papers from the drawer."

"So?"

"I didn't have time to read it all properly, but it sounded like St. Rita's is broke."

"Well, that much doesn't especially surprise me." George shrugged.

"Then it went on to say that charges for the rental of Mrs. McKay's safe deposit box had been 'unpaid for some time' and that she should 'get in touch to arrange payment immediately.'"

"Crikey! So the school is broke, and she's got a deposit box at the bank that got robbed?"

George peeped back round the corner.

"That . . . yes, that appears to be about the size of it," said Daphne.

"Coast's clear," said George, and led Daphne back the way they had come. "It's probably just coincidence. I mean, I can't see Mrs. McKay robbing a bank, but . . ."

"But let's not tell her anything yet, just the same," said Daphne. "Just to be on the safe side."

George ambled to a stop beside one of the large windows with a view out to the grounds at the front of the school. He waved a finger at a familiar car lurching along the driveway. "Well, look who it is."

Daphne looked at who it was.

"Oh! That's the man we saw yesterday. Mr. White. Oh, so he's Mrs. McKay's appointment. *He's* Veronica's uncle?" She frowned. "But what on earth is wrong with his car?"

They walked on to the next window as Mr. White's car continued to judder erratically along the drive.

"Ah!" said George, wincing. "It certainly doesn't look too healthy, does it?"

"Odd, him being here two days running." Daphne led them past the front door and on to a farther window. "I suppose yesterday was business and now today's about Veronica."

They looked on as White got out of the car and gave it an angry kick before walking toward the school's front door.

"Or he's here to complain that certain vital parts of his car seem to have gone missing since the hockey team pulled it out of the hole yesterday," said George. "I told them not to take anything too obvious. Come on. I'd rather he didn't see me, under the circumstances. He doesn't look to be in a very good mood."

They hurried on to the library and found Emily Lime at her desk, drawing some kind of diagram on the top sheet of a pile of paper. She sat up straight and scrutinized her handiwork with a shriveled expression.

"We've got some news," said Daphne.

They told Emily Lime about the letter from the bank.

"So we can't tell Mrs. McKay that we think the intruder's probably coming back in case she's involved somehow." Daphne frowned. "So maybe we should just go to the police. What do you think? I know we've nothing very definite, but if we tell them that Veronica's missing, and there was blood in the corridor, and she wouldn't just leave without her kangaroo . . ."

She already knew how inadequate this sounded, even before she noticed the withering looks that George was giving her.

"No," said Emily Lime. "Of course we don't go to the police." She put down her pencil and stood up. "Obviously we'll have to catch the robber ourselves. Come on, we'll talk it over in the dining hall."

TWENTY-TWO

Daphne, who hadn't eaten anything substantial since the cake Miss Bagley had given her the day before, had been very hungry when they had arrived at the dining hall. When Emily Lime had pushed the door open, Daphne had dashed in, ignoring whatever it was that George had started to say, even though it had sounded really quite urgent.

Then the stench had hit her, like a brick in a fetid sock.

And then she'd found that she was lying on the floor and wondering why her lungs seemed to be on fire again.

Now, sitting at the corner table that Emily Lime and George had dragged her to, with her head thrust out the open window, gulping in gorgeous drafts of cool, fresh air, she could just about believe that she might not, after all, be dying. Her breathing steadied a little and she turned her attention away from trying not to be sick, and noticed that George was talking.

"I did try to warn you," he said. "We haven't ever quite worked out whether Cook is just useless or actually evil, but either way, it's a shock to the system if you're not ready for it. Sorry about that. Are you, er . . . are you feeling any better?"

"A bit," said Daphne, who was surprised to find that her voice now sounded as if she were a thousand years old. "Is it *really* food? I mean . . . the *smell.* It's . . . it's . . ." She shuddered.

"Oh, don't try to describe it. The greatest poets would

fail. Now, give yourself another minute or so and then maybe you can try turning round. Just small breaths when you do, mind. Give yourself a chance to adjust. You do get used to it eventually."

Daphne found this very hard to believe, but after a moment she pulled her head back inside and turned round to sit normally on the bench, vaguely noting that Emily Lime was no longer at the table. She took in a shallow breath and, though the air was thick and vile, she managed not to scream this time. George nodded his approval.

"That's it. Nice and easy. Soon it'll only be horrible instead of excruciating. You're doing really well."

"Everything all right here?" Miss Bagley looked down at Daphne with a sympathetic smile.

"Yes, mmm . . . miss," said George.

"Yes, miss," croaked Daphne. "Just . . ."

"It's not easy, is it, petal? Have you actually eaten anything yet?"

"No, miss."

"Ah. That delight is still to come, eh?" Miss Bagley nodded at George. "And I suppose this idiot didn't think to warn you of these culinary terrors before you came in?"

"I did try—" George began, but Miss Bagley silenced him with a raised hand, like a police constable stopping traffic.

"No. Well, I suppose I ought to have done it myself rather than trust a clot like George to have enough sense. Sorry about that, flower."

Daphne stared up at Miss Bagley's friendly smile. It was a reassuring sight. Perhaps confiding in the deputy head rather than the head would be the thing to do. But how to begin?

"Anyway," said Miss Bagley, "I must dash. I have a meeting with Mrs. McKay. Better not be late." She took a look around the dining hall. "Do try to get the poor girl out of here alive though, won't you, George?"

"Yes, mmm . . . miss," said George.

Miss Bagley gave George a dubious look, then, with a last tight smile to Daphne, headed for the door.

Daphne watched her go, and so took in for the first time the massed ranks of her fellow pupils gathered for lunch.

The scene was much as she'd expected: total mayhem. The younger girls were relatively subdued: loud and unruly, but mostly remaining seated and only occasionally indulging in petty acts of violence. The older girls, though, were wild. There were a number of minor food fights going on, one major fight with no food involved, and an improvised game of hockey using a bread roll as the ball. A chorus line of four sixth years were dancing raucously on top of one table, which was annoying the girls trying to play poker beneath it. It reminded Daphne of the Wild West saloon in a cowboy film she had once seen. There wasn't any whiskey being drunk (so far as she could see) and there didn't seem to be any immediate likelihood of a gunfight, but the sense of rowdy chaos was the same. George seemed entirely unsurprised by it all, though, so she could only assume that this was all very much business as usual.

Emily Lime arrived back at the table with two trays of food, which she set down on the table and began to unload.

"What is it today?" said George.

"See for yourself," said Emily Lime, and pushed a plate over to him.

George took a good look at the contents from several angles, then poked at them with a fork.

"Hmm . . ." he said. "Gray stuff."

Daphne looked down at her own plate as Emily Lime shoved it over to her.

"Gray stuff?" she said. "What sort of gray stuff?"

"Crikey, I don't know," said George. "You'd need to be some sort of scientific genius to work that out." He prodded at the largest item available for inspection. "Some kind of meat, maybe? Or part of a shoe? It's hard to say." His fork rummaged elsewhere amidst something that was a different shade of gray. "And I think this is . . . vegetable-ish." He waved the fork in a circular motion above the whole sorry mess, doused in a liquid that was a third shade of gray. "And it comes with this . . . fluid."

Daphne examined her own plate for comparison.

"Is it gravy?" she said.

George considered this for a moment. "No. I'm going to stick with 'fluid.'"

He leaned in for a closer look, frowned, then straightened up again.

"Lumpy fluid."

They sat there, still amidst the swirling chaos,

gazing at the horrors on their plates. It was the most repulsive food that Daphne had ever seen, but she was hungry enough to give it a try. She raised her fork.

"Hang on," said George. "We haven't said grace yet."

"Oh. Sorry, I didn't realize . . ."

Daphne set down her knife and fork and clasped her hands together. George did likewise, bowed his head, and closed his eyes.

"Lord, save us!" he said, then opened his eyes and glanced at Daphne. "Right, best of luck." With a resigned sigh, he began to eat.

Daphne cut a tiny morsel off the largest gray lump and raised it trembling in front of her face. She looked at it, limp and dripping.

"Now, Lime," said George, in between rapid forkfuls, "about this ridiculous plan of yours . . ."

"It is not ridiculous," said Emily Lime as she sawed at something stubborn on her plate.

"No, of course not. Three weedy schoolchildren—no offense, Daffers—lying in wait for a hardened criminal. Nothing even remotely ridiculous about that!"

Daphne braced herself and began to eat. The first mouthful was the worst thing she had ever tasted. It was bitter and salty and utterly foul. But once she was certain that it hadn't killed her, she forced down a second, which somehow tasted even worse.

"We can be perfectly safe," continued Emily Lime, "so long as we make sensible preparations."

"Preparations?" said George. "How do you mean?"

Daphne drank a glass of water. It did nothing to shift the rank taste in her mouth.

"Obviously we can't hope to overcome our intruder with brute force." Emily Lime stabbed the air with her fork for emphasis. "But while we are, as you so unhelpfully put it, weedy schoolchildren, we are weedy schoolchildren *who read*! And that makes us clever. So we ought to be able to make suitable preparations that will give us an advantage."

Daphne refilled her glass and drained it. The bitter, sour, otherworldly, bad, bad taste in her mouth remained stubbornly undiminished. She looked at her plate and found that, despite having eaten virtually nothing, her appetite had disappeared entirely. She pushed her plate away.

"Do you mean," she croaked, "like a booby trap?"

"No, of course not!" said Emily Lime. "Not *like* a booby trap. *Actually* a booby trap. I jotted down some ideas earlier. Here." Emily Lime held up a bundle of papers, on the top sheet of which Daphne could see a loose and hurried diagram with lots of tiny, messy scribbled notes on it. "See what you think."

It didn't take long to turn into an argument.

"Well, if you've any better ideas, then let's hear them!" said Emily Lime.

"It's not that a scaled-down version of a Roman catapult is a bad idea, exactly," said Daphne (though of course she absolutely thought that it was). "It's just that maybe, in the time we have, something a bit simpler . . ."

". . . that doesn't need us to be experts in carpentry, and to have a load of tools that we haven't got, and to tear apart all the shelves to get enough wood . . ." said George.

". . . might be better," said Daphne.

"Oh, there's always some little detail you pick on, isn't there?"

"Or half a dozen absolutely enormous details," said George. "For every one of your terrible—"

"Not terrible, exactly," said Daphne. "But—"

"Yes, terrible. Yes, exactly," said George. "The laby-
rinth, the trebuchet, the giant spider's web—all of them
are terrible, terrible ideas."

"Well, what," seethed Emily Lime, "do you suggest,
then? If you're so clever, George. What's your brilliant
idea, eh?"

"We knot our ties together and use them as a trip-
wire at the top of the stairs."

Emily Lime thought about this for a moment.

"Yes," she said. "Better."

She gathered up her scribbled diagrams and
returned them to her pockets.

"Have you finished?" She pointed to Daphne's plate,
where the gray gloop bubbled quietly.

"Oh, heavens, yes!" said Daphne.

"You don't want pudding, then?" said George, looking
over to the far right of the serving hatches. "The pud-
dings are less bad."

Daphne gave a small shake of the head.

"No. Fair enough. Probably for the best." He pointed
to the open window. "Now, stick your head out for a
good big breath and then we'll try to get out before you
need another."

He rose from his seat, and he and Emily Lime led Daphne out of the dining hall. The various fights and the hockey game all seemed to have merged into one another now, forming a kind of giant, messy, sporty war, but somehow they found a safe path through it all.

TWENTY-THREE

They had to sit in the dark, of course, huddled on the floor at the foot of the natural history section, out of sight of the door, so that if the intruder came in, then they wouldn't immediately be seen. A little moonlight washed in through the tall windows when the ambling clouds allowed it, drawing hazy shapes in the blackness. They sat in silence—which came naturally to them as librarians—but that silence was not complete. Within the night's quiet, tiny noises seemed to ring out, clear as speech. Every shuffled bottom, every breath, every rumble of George's stomach sounded out as if amplified by the darkness.

The night drifted on, punctuated by rare whispers as one or another of the children checked that the others were still awake, or asked what the latest tiny noise outside might be. Mostly, though, there was silence, stillness, and the dark. Daphne felt at once very bored and very nervous; tired, but surely too tense to sleep.

An expanse of cloud blocked out the moon, and the darkness deepened and bloomed, swallowing up the dim contours of the library. Daphne felt—despite the numb ache in her bottom—as if she were floating in a vast nothingness. She swallowed down her nervousness, and it seemed to her as if the sound of it echoed through the entire school. Her breathing seemed deafening, so she

tried taking tiny, slow breaths, bringing her whole self as close to a stop as she could, slowing her thinking, too, allowing the velvety blackness into her mind. Her anxiety dissolved in the sweet, quiet darkness. She felt as if she, too, were being absorbed into the dark, becoming the night.

The first thing she heard when she woke, after her own startled yelp, was George snoring. She had opened her eyes, but it had made no difference. The library was still full of the same inky darkness, and she could make out nothing at all around her.

She reached a hand out toward the sound of the snoring and gave a prod to what she hoped was George's arm.

"Whuzzah!" said George. Then there was a small *thump*, quickly followed by a larger *THUMP*, then an "Ow!" from George.

"Shh!" said Daphne as Emily Lime woke with a muffled grunt.

"If you want me to shush, then you shouldn't go bloomin' prodding me, should you?" hissed George. "It's bad enough sitting here in the dark without you assaulting me with your pointy fingers for no good reason. You made me knock the book off this shelf. Just my luck that B. F. Hunniman had so much to say about parrots. Landed right on my head, it did. I mean, who needs four hundred and twelve pages of parrots, really?"

"You were snoring," whispered Daphne.

"I was not!" snorted George. "You must have—"

"Shut up!" said Emily Lime. "Listen."

They shut up and they listened.

There was a new noise outside: a scrabbling sound at one of the windows.

"Oh heck!" said George. "We've booby-trapped the door, and they're coming in through the window!"

"But that's not what we planned," said Emily Lime.

"Well, the burglar doesn't know that, does he?" said George. "We'd better come up with a plan B, sharpish."

"Should we run for it?" said Daphne, getting to her feet as quietly as she could. She heard the other two do likewise.

"No," hissed George and Emily Lime at once.

"We should at least get a look at him," said Emily Lime. "As soon as he's in, flashlights on, shine them in his face. He'll be blinded for a second."

"Here, you take mine, Daffers," said George. "I'll chuck the bumper book of parrots at his head."

"Right," gulped Daphne. She took the flashlight from George.

All the bleariness of sleep dispelled now, her senses seemed heightened. She still couldn't see a thing, but she felt every ridge of the grooved casing of the flashlight, the metal cold against her skin; she smelled the must of old books; she heard the tense shallow breaths of her friends and the creak of a half-light window being pushed open.

Feet landed on the wooden floor with a soft thump.

"NOW!" yelled George.

Two beams of light stabbed at the darkness, danced madly around the room like searchlights seeking a target, then converged on the spot that the noise had come from.

"*MRRRROOOW!*" screeched the Beast, flinching from the blinding light and leaping away, dodging George's hurled book and zooming up the physics section to spit feline abuse down at them from the top of the bookcase.

Daphne, George, and Emily Lime gaped up at the monstrous cat, then lowered their flashlights and looked at each other. Then, helpless to resist the wave of relief that washed through them, they laughed. They soon stifled their giggles, but it was still quite some time before they properly regained control of themselves. When they did, Emily Lime was the first to speak.

"Oh, for heaven's sake! Flashlights off!"

"Crikey, yes, of course," said Daphne as she followed Emily's example and returned the library to darkness.

"We'd better hope the intruder wasn't around to see the light," said Emily Lime.

"And that the Beast calms down and doesn't decide to take revenge for half blinding it," whispered George.

"*You'd* better hope it doesn't mind that you tried to brain it with that book," giggled Daphne, handing back his flashlight.

"Ooh, heck!"

"Shush!" said Emily Lime. "Now let's all just settle back down and stay quiet. But without falling asleep this—"

Then the door handle began to turn.

Daphne froze with fear again, every fiber of her being focused on the handle of the library's door, turning with infinite slowness. She realized that the business with the Beast's appearance had left her beyond the shelter of the bookcase. If the intruder turned the light on or shone a flashlight her way, then she would be in clear view.

The door began to open, slowly and far from silently. Amplified by fear and the surrounding silence, its creak seemed like a banshee howl.

Daphne tried to move back behind the shelves, but her legs refused to cooperate. It was as if they had turned to stone. Unable to move her legs, Daphne instead flailed her arms madly. Then a hand caught her arm, gave a tug, and set her moving. Daphne clamped her mouth shut, as tight as the knot of panic in her chest, and tiptoed into hiding.

The door fell silent.

Another pause.

Daphne held a tiny breath.

She heard the first quiet footstep from up by the door. Whoever was there was light on their feet, used to moving silently, she thought. Then another muffled step, a pause, another step, barely audible, then . . .

"AARGH!"

Then a short series of thumps, bumps, and a medium-sized crash.

George's face appeared above the slashing beam of his flashlight.

"Come on!" he said, and led them round the bookcase toward the steps.

A dark-clothed figure lay crumpled on his back at the foot of the steps, looking still and broken. George leapt on top of him, sitting astride his chest like a rodeo rider. Emily Lime climbed on behind him. Daphne briefly contemplated pinning down his knees but judged from the lack of struggle that their captive was out cold. George shone his flashlight at his face.

"Oh!" said George. "It's Mr. Thanet. Well, blimey! I would never've believed he'd be a bank robber."

"Of course he's not, you clot," said Emily Lime. "Look."

Emily Lime panned her flashlight beam over the floor around them, revealing a variety of tools scattered across the boards.

"He wasn't here for the book; he was going to fix the lock on the door."

"At this time of night?" said Daphne. "Are you sure?"

"He's odd like that," said George. "Says he prefers not to disturb lessons in the daytime. Personally I reckon he's just worried about the girls nicking his tools. There's not many of 'em that you'd want to trust with a hammer."

"Oh crikey!" said Daphne. "Now we really are in trouble!"

"You're assuming he's not dead, then?" said Emily Lime.

"What?" yelped Daphne.

"Don't get your knickers in a twist, Daff," said George. "He's still breathing."

Emily Lime made her way up the steps to the door.

"Oh, wonderful," said Daphne. "So at least we're only guilty of *attempted* murder."

"We're not guilty of anything," said Emily Lime, flicking on the lights. "Poor Mr. Thanet tripped down the stairs in the dark." She knelt and began to untie the booby trap. "We weren't even here."

Then the door opened behind her so quickly that the short, sharp creak its hinges made sounded like an *eek* of surprise.

"What the hell," said Cynthia Rawlinson, standing in the doorway with a flashlight clamped in her armpit and a hockey stick in her good hand, "is going on here?"

TWENTY-FOUR

W ell, at least he didn't break any bones," whispered George.

"At least he didn't call the police," Daphne whispered back.

She looked up from the page she was writing, past Emily Lime, seated in the row of desks in front of theirs, to examine the figure of Mrs. O'Connell, lolling in her chair at the front of the classroom.

"Only because Mrs. McKay persuaded him not to," said George. "Fishy, that. But lucky for us, I s'pose."

"Huh!" said Emily Lime, leaning back in her chair to

address George. "And I suppose it's lucky for us we used your idea for a booby trap, too, is it? Otherwise we might have used something that didn't wake half the school."

"Oh, and you were going to fit a silencer to your Roman catapult, I s'pose?"

"Don't try to—"

BANG!

A blackboard eraser crashed onto George's desk, making him shriek, then bounced off and landed somewhere at the back of the room.

Mrs. O'Connell—whom they had all until then assumed to be asleep—rose from her seat at the front of the classroom, her arms braced against her desktop. Her walnut of a face contorted, cracked open, and released a screech.

"YOU WILL ALL BE QUIET!"

And they were quiet.

Mrs. O'Connell sat down again and sipped at her cup of tea. Apparently it wasn't very good, as it made her scowl, etching even more lines into a face already very busy with them. Then her eyelids drooped closed again.

It was four a.m., and they were in detention. It turned out that while Mrs. McKay, the head, was well-known for her reluctance to punish her pupils in normal circumstances, she was more than willing to make an exception when rudely awoken at three o'clock in the morning by Cynthia Rawlinson beating upon her door. Having taken scant notice of the details of the case, Mrs. McKay had dispatched Emily Lime, George, and Daphne to room 101, and woken the aged Mrs. O'Connell to oversee their punishment, then returned to bed.

Mrs. O'Connell, too frail at her great age to dish out the athletic thrashings she had favored in her youth, had settled on setting them to write lines. Specifically, they were to write out, a great many times: *I must not rashly endanger the lives of members of staff, even ones who aren't teachers. And especially not Mr. Thanet, because he's slow enough to get anything done as it is without having broken bones and sprains as an excuse, too.*

George passed Daphne a note. It said: *Do you think she means ten thousand lines between us, or ten thousand each?*

Daphne circled the word *each* and passed the scrap of paper back to George. He was still scowling at it when Daphne nudged his shoulder and passed him another. *Or maybe we're just meant to carry on until we die*, it said.

George considered this a moment, while staring at Mrs. O'Connell. She was now slumped in her chair with her head lolling back and her mouth gaping open, which gave her snoring an impressive bass tone. He scribbled a reply and passed back Daphne's note.

I don't think Mrs. O'C would let us off that lightly.

They distractedly wrote a few more lines, their pen nibs scratching away. Emily Lime, meanwhile, sitting in the row in front of them, set down her pen and observed for a moment the bead of drool gathering at the corner of Mrs. O'Connell's mouth. It trembled with each new snore. When, at last, it broke free and set off down the ancient teacher's chin, Emily Lime stood and turned to the others.

"Right, come on," she said.

"Oh!" said George.

"We can't just go!" said Daphne. She cast a worried look at Mrs. O'Connell. "Even if she definitely is asleep now, there's no way of knowing—"

"Oh, she's asleep all right," said George. He gave Emily Lime a stare. "I just hope you got the dosage right this time."

"The dosage . . . ?"

"Oh, for goodness' sake, George," said Emily. "I'm not going to make the same mistake again, am I? She'll only be out for a couple of hours."

"You . . . You've drugged a teacher?" Daphne's eyes were wide with surprise.

"Yes, yes," said Emily Lime. "A little bit. Hardly at all. Don't go making a fuss. It's bad enough that George—"

"Brilliant!" said Daphne. "What did you use?"

"Oh." It was Emily Lime's turn to look surprised. "It's pretty basic. Chloral hydrate. Nothing fancy, but it's effective enough."

"I see. How did you get hold of it?"

"I made it myself in the chemistry lab, actually. I read how to do it in a book. It's not so hard. I usually keep a dose or two in my pencil case just in case." She stood up and began to gather up her papers: the few with lines written on, and the many blank sheets, too. "Now come on. And bring your lines."

"I see," said Daphne as she stood. "And I suppose you slipped it into the teacup when you went to sharpen your pencil at her desk. I thought that was odd, when you were writing in ink. But isn't the taste a bit obvious in tea?"

"Ah, well, Old Oakface generally has a nip of something in her tea, anyway," said George. "She thinks no one notices, but the whole school knows about it. It more or less masks the taste." He tilted his head at Emily. "So long as you don't use too much."

"Oh, do stop it, George. Miss Blenkinsop was perfectly fine, as you well know." She crossed her arms tightly. "Eventually."

"After she came out of the coma, you mean?"

"You put a teacher in a coma?" said Daphne.

"Just a little one," said Emily Lime. "And actually I think the rest did her good. She'd been overworking, and lost a lot of weight. That's probably why I miscalculated the dosage."

"Yes," said George. "That'll be it. Nothing to do with the fact that you can't do math for toffee."

"I can work out that if you keep wittering on, then we won't have time to do everything we need to before Mrs. O'Connell wakes up again," said Emily Lime. "So let's just drop the subject and get on, shall we?"

She held out a hand, and George handed her all his papers. "Yours, too, new girl. Hand over your papers, and I'll deal with your lines for you."

Daphne, puzzled, passed Emily Lime her sheaf of papers.

"Go to the library. I'll join you soon," said Emily Lime, starting toward the door. "We'll take another look at that book."

As Daphne stood to follow, she took a last look at Mrs. O'Connell. She had slumped so far down in her chair now that only her head was visible above desk height. Her rasping snores sent ripples through the top sheet of the papers she had brought along to mark.

"She will wake up, won't she?" said Daphne.

"Oh yes," said George, shuffling along behind her. "Almost certainly. Eventually."

TWENTY-FIVE

While Emily Lime herself made virtually no noise at all as she stepped into the library, the door was altogether less considerate, and creaked loudly as it swung open. George and Daphne, slumped asleep, *Scarlet Fury* lying open on the table between them, sprang awake, startled by the noise.

"Well, that's the lines taken care of," said Emily Lime. "What progress have you made while I've been gone?"

"Oh," said Daphne blearily. "Well, er, we've been looking at the book, and . . ."

"And?"

"And we haven't found a thing. We must be missing something. . ."

"I'm missing my bed," said George.

". . . but we can't even think straight. We're just too tired."

"Oh yes. Well, I thought of that."

Emily Lime placed a thermos and two mugs on the table.

"I stopped in at the kitchen on the way back and made us some coffee."

She unscrewed the cup from the top of the thermos and placed it next to the mugs, then poured out three generous measures of a treacly black liquid.

"Coffee?" said George.

"I've never had coffee before," said Daphne. "But is it meant to look like that? Shouldn't it be . . . runnier?"

"I don't think so," said Emily Lime. "I put twice as much water in as coffee as it is. If I made it any weaker I can't imagine it would help us to stay awake at all."

George took a sip and screwed his face up.

"Gyuurrgh! That's disgusting! Do grown-ups really drink this stuff for fun?"

"Apparently," said Daphne. "Maybe it's an acquired— eeurgh—taste."

"I can't see how it can be worth the effort," said George, hovering his cup under his wrinkled nose as he contemplated a second try.

"Well, you wouldn't, I suppose," said Emily Lime. "You lack the sophistication."

Then she supped a mouthful of the murky liquid with exaggerated daintiness.

And spat it out.

"Well," said George. "I can only dream of one day being as sophisticated as you, Your Majesty. In the meantime, I'll go and find a cloth."

As George mopped up coffee from the table, the floor, and the anthropology shelf, Emily Lime leafed through *Scarlet Fury*.

"What are we looking for?" said Daphne.

Emily Lime screwed up her face, took a determined (but tiny) sip of her coffee, and, grimacing, swallowed it down.

"No idea," she said. "But the answer to any problem is always in a book."

George finished his mopping up and joined them at the table. Seeing Daphne swallow down another tiny gulp of coffee, he gave his own mug another sip.

"Gah! Couldn't you at least have put some sugar in this rotten stuff, Lime?"

Emily Lime looked up from the book.

"Eh? Oh, I wasn't sure if you were meant to. But I brought some along in case. Here."

She stood up and turned out one of the pockets of her pinafore, depositing a mound of white crystals onto the table. Then she did the same with her other pocket. The result was a decent-sized molehill of sugar, albeit speckled with fluff, scraps of paper, and a boiled sweet.

"Couldn't you have put—" began Daphne, but George and Emily Lime were already brushing sugar off the edge of the table and into their cups, and Daphne didn't want to miss out on her share. She plopped about half of what was left into her mug and stirred it in with a pencil. Then, after another face-mangling sip, she added the rest. Her next taste was somehow disgustingly sweet and appallingly bitter at the same time, but on the whole, slightly less awful than the last. Daphne thought she could probably just about get through the whole cup if she really tried, though she didn't see the point. It wasn't as if it was making her any more awake.

Half an hour later, they had, between them, seen off the entire thermos. Now they were gathered at the table as Emily Lime sat speeding through *Scarlet Fury* for the sixth time, and Daphne and George peered over either

shoulder. Emily Lime flipped the pages with one hand while the other raked through her hair.

"There MUST be something we're missing," she gabbled. Her eyes were very wide and seemed to be vibrating. She got to the end of *Scarlet Fury* yet again and immediately started flipping through the pages a seventh time, this time even faster than before and backward.

"Backward?" George frowned at the turning pages as they sped by.

"Looking at it from another angle," said Emily Lime.

"Mmm—makes sense," said George with a violent shrug, then climbed onto the other side of the table on his hands and knees, craning his head so that his eyes were just above the pages as they flickered by. "I'll try upside down, too." His hands were clamped round the edges of the table, his knuckles white. "Maybe we need more COFFEE," said George. "Do you think we need more coffee? I think we need more coffee! Then we'll see. Then we'll really see!"

"Yes! The last lot wasn't strong enough," said Daphne, circling the table at a frantic pace and swishing her arms about as if trying to wave away a swarm of invisible flies.

"Yes. More coffee. Then I could speak as quickly as I'm thinking," gabbled Emily Lime. "So frustrating having to talk so slowly, don't you think?"

"Yes, it is," said George and Daphne both at once and very quickly.

George's eyes looked fit to pop. Daphne did a U-turn and started circling the table the other way.

"Perhaps there's a coded message in the story," said Emily Lime. "I read some books on codes once. I've tried first letters of each sentence, each chapter, every thirteenth letter, and twenty-three other possibilities, but nothing's worked so far."

"I don't care what you try, just turn the pages faster!" said George, though they were already riffling by so quickly that his hair was dancing in the breeze they created.

"I have to go this slowly to be thorough," said Emily, almost back at the beginning already.

"Can't be a code," said Daphne. "The book was printed before the robbery happened. How can there be a clue in it about a robbery that hadn't happened yet?"

"I don't know," said George. "But there must be. The key to this whole business is in this book somewhere.

And if I just stare at it for another hour or so, I'm sure I'll see it."

His head began to shake, tiny fast tremors that quickly spread first to his arms and then to his body and legs.

"Stop that!" said Emily Lime. "You're rocking the table. How can I concentrate when you're rocking the table?"

"How am *I* meant to concentrate when you're so slow?"

Daphne was distracted by another thought.

"Do you remember when we used to blink? All the time, closing and opening our eyes? Why did we do that? What a waste of time!"

She stopped circling the table and set off on a new, seemingly random trajectory, jerkily stuttering along a haphazard course like a distracted housefly.

"Or maybe if we look at every letter that comes just after an exclamation mark," said Emily Lime.

"It's not a code!" said Daphne, bouncing off a distant bookcase and heading off in a fresh direction like a bumper car.

George was shaking so hard now that his fists and knees were rattling the table.

"Stop that!" said Emily Lime.

"Stop what?" gibbered George, his voice wobbling in time with the ever more violent convulsions of his body. "I'm not, I'm not, I'm not . . ." He trailed off as the vibrations calmed to a gentle wobble, but all color left his face. When he spoke again, it was slowly and deliberately.

"Oh," he said. "I don't feel . . . too clever."

"Well, *that's* hardly news," said Emily Lime.

"No . . . I mean . . ."

Emily Lime looked up into George's pale face and saw very clearly what was coming.

"Don't be sick," she said. "Don't you dare be sick in my library!"

"And not on the book!" said Daphne, speeding back toward the table, her arms outstretched.

"Oh . . ." said George.

Emily Lime snapped the book closed just as Daphne arrived at the table and grabbed hold of it.

"Ooh . . ." said George.

Daphne lifted the book toward her. Emily Lime pulled it back.

"Oh dear . . ." said George.

"Let go!" said Emily Lime.

"*You* let go!" said Daphne.

George groaned.

"Give it to me!" Emily Lime wrenched the book from Daphne's hands.

George drew in a wheezing breath and clutched at his stomach.

Free of Daphne's grip, the book hit Emily Lime hard in the chest, then flew up into the air.

"OOOOH!" moaned George.

Daphne and Emily Lime each grasped at the book, caught hold of a cover, and pulled. There was a horrible tearing sound, and the clatter of two schoolgirls falling onto a wooden floor, then the undelightful rasp of George throwing up.

And a small metallic ting.

"Well, that feels much better," said George, climbing down from the table and dabbing at his smiling mouth with the end of his tie. "I'll go and fetch that cloth again."

Daphne stood up, feeling groggy and dizzy. She no longer felt like racing around the room. In fact, standing still seemed like rather a challenge now. Her head was aching, too.

"I'm not sure coffee really agrees with me," she said as she leaned heavily against the table for support. Her head lolled forward, and she noted the soothing pattern of the wood grain in the floorboards. But there was something breaking the pattern. Something small and shiny and out of place. She bent down to pick it up.

"Oh, what's this?" she said.

It was a key.

TWENTY-SIX

It's a key," said Daphne. She held it out for inspection by the others.

George glanced at it on his way back to the table.

"Not mine," he said, and cheerfully set about wiping coffee-colored gloop into the wastepaper basket.

Emily Lime, scowling as she rubbed at the part of her bottom that had recently hit the floor, gave a dismissive grunt.

"But where did it . . . ?"

Daphne lowered her hand. Her head was getting back to normal now. The effects of the coffee and the

sugar had more or less worn off and now that she had
something to think about, her brain was doing its best
to rise to the challenge. She looked away from the key
and saw the ragged half of a book in her other hand.

"Oh dear," she said. "What have we . . ." She stopped
short. "Oh, hello."

She pointed at the inside of the spine. Attached to
the book cloth there was a large glob of some sort of
white resin.

George looked up from wiping the tabletop.

"They made a mess of gluing it together, didn't they? That's a right botched job."

"Don't try to blame the glue!" said Emily Lime, stabbing a finger in Daphne's direction. "It's this maniac's fault that it's come apart! What did you think you—oh!"

There was an indentation in the hardened blob of glue. Daphne laid the key against it, and it fit perfectly.

"Crikey!" said George. "Well, I said the key to this mystery was in the book, but I didn't mean it literally."

"It's a funny-looking thing though, isn't it?" said Daphne. "Unusual shape, I mean. Oh, and there's a number on it. See?" She held it up again. "336."

"Well, it's not for any of the classrooms," said George. "They jump straight from 331 to Z. Does 336 mean anything to you, Lime?"

"Public finance," said Emily Lime. "Obviously."

"What?"

"336: Economics/Public finance."

George rolled his eyes. "I don't think the Dewey decimal system has anything to do with it."

"You know, I'm pretty sure it's not a door key," said Daphne.

George took a closer squint.

"I'm pretty sure you're right. But Peters would know for sure."

"Oh yes. How is it she's so good with locks, anyway?"

"Picked it up from her dad, I s'pose."

"Oh, is he a locksmith?"

"No, a safe breaker." George took the key from Daphne. "I'll go and see her. Meet you back in detention. You say you've got our lines all sorted out, Lime?"

"Yes. I'll fetch them. Meet me back in 101." She made her way out.

"And what should *I* do?" said Daphne.

George handed her the wastepaper basket as he breezed past.

"You can empty this out, if you like."

He was nearly at the door as the acrid smell reached Daphne's nose and she shriveled her face in disgust.

"Ew!"

"Might need a bit of a rinse, too," said George. "Quick about it, mind; Mrs. O'Connell should be waking up soon." Then he was gone before Daphne had a chance to reply.

At a quarter past six, Daphne and Emily Lime arrived from opposite directions at the door to room 101. As

Emily Lime's hands were full with a bundle of paper, Daphne opened the door, slowly and silently, and pushed it open. As they crept in, George clumped in behind them.

"Hey!" he said. "You'll never guess—"

"Sh!" Emily Lime silenced him with a powerful glare.

"Sorry," whispered George.

They looked over at Mrs. O'Connell's desk. There was no sign of Mrs. O'Connell.

"Oh crikey!" said Daphne. "Where's she—"

"Lime! You idiot!" said George. "First you overdose a teacher, now you've underdosed one! She'll be prowling the corridors looking for us. Now we're—"

A deep, loud snore, like the sound of a double bass being sawn in half, split the air. The children crept over to Mrs. O'Connell's desk and found, behind it, Mrs. O'Connell slumped on the floor, her mouth gaping open and a thin line of drool trailing from one corner.

"You were saying?" said Emily Lime, and led them back to their seats, then divided up her bundle of papers into three substantial piles and handed one each back to Daphne and George. Daphne leafed through her pile, astonished at the dense lines of script on each page.

"This is my handwriting!" she said.

"Of course," said Emily Lime. "Ten thousand lines exactly."

"But how . . . ?"

George grinned.

"Hibbitt, was it?" he said. "And then Hewlett, I suppose?"

"Yes," said Emily Lime.

"Hibbitt's a nifty little forger in the lower sixth," explained George. "She writes out three or four pages based on your writing; then Hewlett has a lovely little press set up for counterfeiting—her parents used to do ration cards—and she duplicates however many you need."

He nosed through his own sheaf. "Blimey, though, these are works of art. I'd almost swear that I'd written these."

Then he frowned. "Hey, they're not cheap, though. What's this cost us, Lime?"

"Double their usual rate for the unsociable hours, and then double again for it being a rush job," said Emily Lime.

"Oh, and how are we meant to pay for that?" said George.

"You'll think of something."

"I s'pose I shall have to. Oh, but about the key—"

"Hang on," said Daphne, nodding toward the front of the room.

From beneath the desk, the steady rhythm of Mrs. O'Connell's snoring transformed first into a broken series of snorting grunts, and then into silence. Emily Lime turned to face forward in her seat, disarranged her stack of pages, and then lifted her pen and adopted a studious pose. George and Daphne followed her lead as Mrs. O'Connell, her hair hilariously askew, emerged from beneath her desk and climbed back up into her chair with what little dignity she could muster. The children pretended they hadn't noticed.

After a little poorly disguised stretching and yawning, Mrs. O'Connell took a shifty glance at her watch, gave her teacup a hard stare of reproach, and cleared her throat to speak.

"Hrrummf. That will do for now, girls. Erm, and George. Go and get some breakfast now. You may return after supper this evening to continue—"

"Er, 'scuse me, miss," said George, standing up, "but actually we've already finished."

He started toward Mrs. O'Connell's desk with his pile of papers.

"Now, George, please don't be silly. You're in quite enough trouble as it is without—"

"But he has, miss," said Emily Lime. "We all have."

She and Daphne got up and followed George to the front of the class.

"Yes," said George. "We really knuckled down to it, didn't we, girls? Here you go, miss."

George deposited his lines on the teacher's desk, then Emily Lime and Daphne added theirs on top, then they all started toward the door.

"Hang on just a moment!" called Mrs. O'Connell in a commanding voice, and the children ground to a halt.

Daphne's heart sank.

Mrs. O'Connell leafed through the sheets of lines for a moment, then nodded and smiled.

"There's ten thousand lines from each of us there, miss. Honest," said George.

"I don't doubt it for a moment." Mrs. O'Connell looked up at the children with a knowing smile. "And that, happily, means none of us need come back here again, for which I'm very grateful. So off you all go."

"Thank you, miss," chorused the children.

"And tell Hibbitt and Hewlett well done from me, and I shall expect my usual cut by the end of the week."

*

"So, the key . . ." said George once they had gotten a few paces away from room 101 and the ears of Mrs. O'Connell.

Daphne caught the excitement in his voice. "Oh yes? What did Peters say?"

"She's pretty sure it's for a safe-deposit box."

"Crikey!" said Daphne. "At the Pilkington District Bank?"

"She couldn't tell, but . . . well, it's got to be, hasn't it?"

"No," said Emily Lime.

Daphne's face fell.

They walked on in silence for a moment as an early clump of girls dashed past them toward the dining hall.

"No, it doesn't *have* to be," said Emily Lime. Her mouth twitched at the corners in what Daphne took to be a rather amateur attempt at a smile. "But it certainly could be."

"But if the book belonged to whoever robbed the bank," said George, "then why would they have a key to a safe-deposit box? The boxes that were robbed were broken open, not just unlocked."

"What did that reprobate nun say?" said Emily Lime.

Daphne cast her mind back. "She said . . . that the tricky thing with a robbery is hiding what you've stolen."

"That's right," said Emily Lime.

"So if our robber had a key . . ."

Emily Lime nodded, and her mouth twitched again.

". . . then what better place to hide the loot than in another one of the boxes?" Daphne's mouth dropped open.

"Oh, that's clever." George gave an appreciative nod. "So long as you don't lose the key."

"But if that is what happened," said Daphne, "and *we* have the key . . . then what do we *do*? Do we call the police?"

"Hang that," said George.

"But—"

"Yes," said Emily Lime. "Hang that. We go to the bank."

TWENTY-SEVEN

As the rest of the school made their way to morning assembly, Emily Lime, Daphne, and George dodged and swerved in the opposite direction, through a surging mass of girls, to the library, and then out the back way. They "borrowed" bicycles to ride to Pelham station, and George got return tickets to Pilkington for them all.

Daphne and George slept the entire journey, then, after polishing off some sandwiches from the tea shop, slept through the short bus ride into town, too. Emily Lime almost had to drag them out at their stop.

"Which way now?" Daphne's neck ached from the awkward position she had slept in.

"Follow me." Emily Lime set out across the road.

Daphne yawned and tried to massage the pain in her neck away as she and George stepped off the sidewalk. A small boy in an oversized flat cap riding an oversized bicycle careered between them on the wrong side of the road, delivering a glancing blow to George as he went.

"Hey! Watch where you're going! Clot!" yelled George.

The boy glanced back at them and stuck his tongue out, then disappeared into a startled crowd of pensioners.

The rest of their short walk was mercifully undramatic, and they soon arrived at a crossroads, where Emily Lime brought them to a halt.

"There it is," said Emily Lime.

Daphne and George followed her gaze to the building on the corner diagonally opposite.

"Oh!" said Daphne. "So that's it, then. The Pilkington District Bank: our destination; our destiny; the scene of the crime!"

They looked at it some more. The door opened, and a boring-looking man in a boring-looking raincoat came out of the boring-looking door.

"It looks a bit . . . boring, doesn't it?" said George.

"It really does," said Daphne. "So, um . . . what do we do now?"

"Obviously we go in and take a look at the safe-deposit boxes," said Emily Lime. "And, assuming there's a box number 336, George can see if the key fits."

"Eh?" said George, looking less than delighted.

"But how can we even get them to let us in to where the boxes are?" said Daphne. "It's not long since they were robbed, so they're probably being extra careful now. And I don't suppose they like schoolchildren much, especially ones from St. Rita's."

"No," said Emily Lime. "But you know who banks do like?"

"Um, no," said Daphne.

"Rich people," said Emily Lime.

"But we're not—"

"No," said Emily Lime, "but . . ." She took off her beret,

coughed twice, and gathered herself. When she spoke again her voice was hearty and brash. "But we know someone who jolly well is."

"Cripes!" said Daphne. "That's very good! You sound *just* like Marion!"

"Yes. I read a book about impressions once—by mistake, don't you know? Thought it was going to be about impressionist painters, you see. Ha! Silly mistake, but, hey ho! I read it anyway and, wouldn't you know it, turns out I'm rather a natural!"

"I don't see how this helps," grumbled George.

"No? Well, chin up, Georgie boy! Let's all tootle over and I'll show you!"

And with that, she marched across the road toward the bank. Daphne and George exchanged shrugs and trailed along in her wake.

There were two lines inside the bank. Emily Lime strode to the front of the longer one.

"Excuse me!" said the annoyed-looking woman at the front of the line.

"Oh really, my dear old thing," said Emily Lime without looking round, "don't mention it." She raised a finger at the cashier. "Hello there! How do you do, and all that rot. Need to have a chinwag with someone about opening an account. Thought maybe you could help."

The cashier gaped at her, unable to form a suitable response.

"Now, look here, young lady," said the furious-looking woman at the front of the line. Emily Lime ignored her.

The cashier spoke at last, in a quiet, tremulous voice.

"Actually, miss, I'm afraid—"

"Afraid? Really? Whatever of? Actually, second thoughts, don't tell me. In a bit of a hurry, so don't really have time to discuss your phobias. Name's Fink. Marion Fink."

"Well, Miss Fink, if you could just—"

"Of the Worcestershire Finks."

"Oh yes?"

"Yes. Daddy owns half."

"I'm sorry?"

"I said my father owns half."

"Half of what?"

"Worcestershire. Since the divorce, anyway. Mummy's lawyer was *terribly* good."

"Excuse me, Walter." The cashier for the other line leaned in over the first's shoulder. "Hello, miss. Digby Canning, assistant manager. Did you say *Fink*? We weren't expecting you until . . . Tuesday next week, wasn't it?"

"Well, yes, but I had to come into town today. Bit of shopping to do for my friend Cicely's birthday. So I thought, while I was in the vicinity, I might as well drop by. Do you mind?"

"Excuse me just one moment," said Digby Canning. Then he returned to his own station and placed a *Position Closed* notice on the counter. Back at Walter's shoulder, he raised his voice a little to be heard above the building rumble of resentment from the lines.

"If you'd just like to step this way, miss." He grinned

the widest and oiliest grin in the world, and waved a hand to indicate a door to the left of the counter.

"Oi!" A burly man in overalls glared at Canning. "What about us, then?"

"My colleague will be delighted to assist you in due course, sir," said Digby Canning, dropping the grin and waving a hand toward the back of Walter's line. Then he zipped over to the door. By the time he opened it, the smile was back on, full beam.

"How can I be of assistance, miss?" he said, and extended a limp hand that Emily Lime ignored.

"Hope you don't mind, but I brought along a couple of chums." Emily Lime summoned George and Daphne with a jerk of her head. "Afraid my math is just awful, so I brought along these bright sparks to help out with the numbers side of things."

"Oh, that's, um . . . that's fine," said Digby Canning as they marched past him and through the door. "May I get you all some tea?"

"Oh, no, don't bother," said Emily Lime. "Such a small matter. I don't suppose we'll be long."

"All I need is an account for my allowance to be paid into," said Emily Lime as Daphne and George sat on the two chairs facing Canning's desk. Emily Lime stood beside them. "Only a thousand a month . . ."

Digby Canning seemed for a moment to have lost control of his legs, eyes, and voice. He wobbled, stared, and stammered.

"A thuh . . . A thousand?" he said. "Um, let me get you a chair."

Mr. Canning brought round the chair from behind his desk, dusted it with his handkerchief, and gestured for Emily Lime to sit on it.

"Oh, thanks awfully," said Emily Lime. "Jolly kind of you."

Mr. Canning went back to his desk and extracted a sheet of paper from one of the drawers. "Of course, Miss Fink, you would be entitled to our special Executive Account."

He brought the sheet round and offered it to Emily Lime. "You'll see the terms are much more agreeable than those of our standard account. You see? The figures at the top of the page?"

George snatched the sheet from his fingers. "Thanks very much. Now, let's take a gander . . ."

Canning gave a brief frown, then backed off to perch on the edge of his desk.

"I see," said George.

Daphne watched him as he pursed his lips in pretend concentration, furrowed his brow, and generally did his best to look as if he knew anything at all about the numbers on the paper. Daphne didn't think he looked very convincing, and by the look of things, Mr. Canning didn't think so either. But why would he? Daphne felt a flutter of worry in her stomach. Surely they were about to be found out. Unless . . .

"Daphne, take a look at this, will you?" George handed over the paper.

Daphne cast an eye over the list of figures. They reminded her of one of the particularly boring bits of the newspaper she had read on the train. Perhaps, if she could just be bold enough . . .

George whispered in her ear: "Just try to look like you know—"

"Oh," said Daphne. "Well, this won't do at all!" She jabbed at the sheet of paper with an indignant finger. "This interest rate would have been wholly inadequate even before the Bank of England's recent increase in the base rate. And your overdraft terms are simply laughable. The Mulverston Provident, to name but one, offers far superior terms. If this is really the best you can do, then I'm afraid Miss Fink will have to take her business elsewhere."

Daphne stared up at Mr. Canning, concentrating hard on not blinking. Mr. Canning stared straight back in reassuring astonishment.

"Er, well, I shall have to check with my manager. I, um . . . I don't have the authority . . . And I'm afraid he's not here just at the moment, but, er . . . he should be in shortly. Then we, um . . ."

"Well," said Emily Lime, "tell you what. While we're waiting, there *was* one other thing . . ."

"Oh yes?" Mr. Canning turned his attention to Emily Lime, and Daphne breathed a tiny, silent sigh of relief.

"Got quite a few valuables, you know," said Emily Lime. "Presents from Ma and Pa, and so on. Couple of bits and pieces from sultans and maharajahs. You know the sort of thing. Worth an absolute packet. And the girls at St. Rita's—well, they're a lovely bunch, but just a bit . . . criminal. So I was wondering if I could keep some of the tastier items safe and sound here?"

"Well, of course we do have a highly secure vault, and safe-deposit boxes."

"Safe-deposit boxes! Just the jolly old ticket! Lovely safe boxes to deposit things in. Perfect. Can we see?"

"Er, well . . ." Mr. Canning frowned uncertainly. "Normally the manager . . ."

Daphne tutted.

"Er, but under the circumstances," said Mr. Canning, "I'm sure we can make an exception."

Mr. Canning slid clumsily off his desk, and led the children out of the office and through another door, which Mr. Canning unlocked with a large brass key. Daphne followed the others as they descended a flight of stairs to a shiny metal door with a large wheel at its center and a dial to one side. Canning fiddled with the dial, concealing it from view like a schoolboy hiding his paper in an exam, then turned the wheel and pulled, and the door swung open.

"As you see"—Canning rapped on the door with his fist—"this is ten-inch-thick steel. Extremely secure. Now, if you'd like to follow me . . ."

Daphne shivered as she followed the others in. It was a long, thin rectangular space, leading away from the door through which they had entered. The walls contained

columns of metal doors—hundreds of them—of various sizes.

"All the boxes are equally sturdy and secure, and our customers are, of course, guaranteed absolute discretion in their use."

The children had split up and were slowly wandering around the room making a show of inspecting the place with a critical eye.

"Hmm . . . they seem adequate, I suppose," said Daphne, examining the box she was closest to. It was number 93.

"I think they're rather jolly!" said Emily Lime. Daphne looked past her to the number of the box she was looking at: 203. "Bit dinky, though."

"Oh, well," said Mr. Canning, "we offer a range of sizes, according to our customers' needs. The largest ones are—"

"Over here!" said George rather too excitedly.

Daphne turned, with the others, to look. George was pointing straight at box 336, then he opened his hand and included the rest of the wall in a florid wave.

"Um, one of these'd do, wouldn't it, Em-mmm . . . Marion?"

"Oh yes! Those are much more the ticket," said Emily Lime. "Probably need a couple, I should think."

She wandered to the far side of Mr. Canning to draw his attention away from George.

"Some of the gold statues are alarmingly big, I'm afraid. Jolly pretty, of course, but not very practical."

Canning nodded, then took a nervous glance at George. Daphne put herself in his way and made a concerned sort of noise.

"Some of these boxes," she said, pointing to one as far from George as possible, "look newer than the others." She wandered past Canning and was relieved to find that he followed her. "Why is that?" She turned to face him with an intense stare that she hoped would hold his attention.

Far behind Canning, George was loitering by box 336 with the key poised.

"Um, we . . . *upgraded* some of the boxes," said Canning. "To make them more . . . that is, *even* more . . . secure."

Daphne nodded.

"Only *some* of the boxes?" she said. Her mouth was dry with nerves, which made her voice cracked and quiet.

Canning leaned in closer to hear her.

"Er, yes," he said.

"Why is that? Why not all the boxes? Do you give some of your customers preferential treatment?" Daphne's eyes flicked over to peek at George, who had discovered that box 336, like all the boxes, had two keyholes. He tried the key in the first one.

"Oh, no," said Canning. "Of course not."

Daphne glanced at George again. He had abandoned the first keyhole and was trying the second.

"Oh," said Daphne. "So you'd treat Marion Fink, the daughter of Lord Fink of Collingmere, Fifth Viscount of Bimblehurst, just like any of your other customers?"

"Oh, no!" Canning blustered "No. Of course Miss Fink would get our very best service."

Don't look at George, she told herself. She needed to hold Canning's attention and keep him from looking round. *Whatever you do, don't look at George.* But, for heaven's sake, how long did it take to turn a key? *Don't look at George!*

She looked at George.

He appeared to have engaged box 336 in a wrestling match. And he seemed to be losing. The briefest flicker of alarm passed over Daphne's face. Canning saw it, gave a puzzled squint, and began to turn. Daphne's mouth dropped open in silent horror.

"Oho!" said Emily Lime, who was suddenly distractingly close to Mr. Canning and pointing an attention-demanding finger almost into his eye. "So you don't give your very best service to all your customers, then, Mr. Digby Canning? That's a bit rum. One service for the hoi polloi and another for the aristocracy, eh? Is that the kind of ship you're running here?"

"Well, I . . . that is . . ." Canning's voice was steeped in panic now.

Daphne looked past him, to see George stepping away from box 336 and shrugging apologetically.

"Well, I'm very glad to hear it!" boomed Emily Lime. "Need your very best security, not the cut-rate version you dish out to the riffraff."

"Oh, well, actually the security really is the same for all our customers. We use the same two-key system for all the boxes, and—"

"*Two* keys?" said Daphne, rather too shrilly.

"Yes. The customer has one key, and we keep the other. So neither the customer nor the bank can open the box alone."

"Oh," said Daphne, feeling, and sounding, rather deflated.

"Ahem," said Mr. Canning. "Does that sound satisfactory?"

"Well," said Emily Lime, already moving toward the door at some speed, "that all sounds just the ticket."

George and Daphne fell into line behind her.

"But we need to push off now. Tight schedule. Things to do. We'll toddle back next week and sort out all the details."

"Oh, er . . . of course," said Canning, skipping ahead of them to reopen the vault door. "And then I'm sure our manager will be very glad to meet you personally."

"That'll be just dandy! Can't wait!" said Emily Lime, setting off up the stairs.

"We'll let you know," said Daphne. She realized she couldn't wait to be out of the bank. She felt so foolish. Her face screwed tight, and close to tears, she climbed the stairs, her gaze fixed on the oblong of light at the top. Then a figure appeared, silhouetted in the light.

"Oh!" said Canning. "Just in time."

The figure withdrew to allow Emily Lime to get by.

"So sorry I wasn't here when you arrived."

Daphne wondered why the voice sounded familiar.

"I was just coming down, but no doubt Mr. Canning has told you all you need to know about our facilities."

"Oh yes," said Emily Lime as Daphne came through the doorway behind her. "We've had the full tour, all right. I should say so."

Emily Lime made as if to swerve straight past the new

arrival, but he smoothly tethered her with a handshake. As he did so, Daphne got a clear look at him and realized at once why his voice had seemed familiar. His tall, slim frame was unmistakable, and his hair, slick with hair oil, did not look so different now from when it had been soaking wet from a downpour. And he seemed almost as flustered. A wayward lock of hair fell down over one eye as Emily Lime reluctantly shook his hand.

"Marion Fink," said Emily Lime. "Over the moon to meet you, old fruit, but I'm afraid—"

"Ian White," said Mr. White. "I'm the manager here, for my sins. Please excuse me if I look a little . . . disheveled."

He released Emily Lime's hand and scraped his hair roughly back into place. "I'm afraid my motorcar has been rather temperamental lately, and today it decided to give up the ghost comp . . ." His voice trailed off as he noticed Daphne and George loitering by the door to the stairway. His face registered puzzlement, then dawning recognition.

"And these," said Canning, waving a hand at Daphne and George, "are, um . . ."

"We've actually already met, haven't we?" said Mr. White, his eyes narrowing.

"Yes. At the school," said Daphne, with a forced smile. "Nice to see you again, sir."

White's hand, slick with oil from his hair, clasped Daphne's, and she couldn't stop herself from shivering slightly.

"Oh, of course." Mr. White kept hold of Daphne's hand. His eyes bore into hers. She felt her throat tighten. "Miss Fink is very fortunate, I'm sure, to have you looking after her best interests."

He angled his head just a fraction, holding her gaze, his face tight and unnerving. Then George barged between them, offering up his own hand, and forcing White to release Daphne from his clammy grip.

"Well, you've got that right," said George, grabbing and instantly releasing White's hand as Daphne slipped away. "Marion's bloomin' useless without us." He ducked away after Daphne, who, with Emily Lime, was making for the exit with unconcealed haste.

"Quite true, I'm afraid," Emily Lime called back. "Anyway, it's toodle-oo for now. But we'll see you next week."

"Of course," said Mr. White, striding after them. "Here, let me see you out."

He sped past them to the door back to the main body of the bank, grabbed hold of the handle, but made no move to turn it. He fixed his eyes on Emily Lime's. "And I do hope your cold will have cleared up by then."

Emily Lime frowned. "Cold? What makes you think I have a cold? I'm right as ninepence."

"Oh, sorry. It's just that you sounded different on the telephone." His lips pursed.

Daphne stared at his hand on the door handle, willing him to turn it. She tried to swallow, but she felt as if the cloying air had blocked her throat. She wondered if she was about to be sick.

"Perhaps just my memory playing tricks," said White, at last, and opened the door, gesturing toward it. "Please," he said, then remained there, looming over them with polite menace as they filed out.

Daphne forced herself not to look back as they made their way across the floor. Walking felt like an unfamiliar and complex task, and she felt sure her legs would give way beneath her, but at the same time she desperately wanted to break into a run. Then she felt a hand close briefly around hers.

"Steady, Daffers," whispered George, by her side. "Steady."

They looked at each other, exchanged tight smiles, and walked on past the lines of customers until, at last, they were out. The fresh air and sunlight hit Daphne hard enough that she nearly crumpled, but George took her hand again and led her on, after Emily Lime, across the road and round a corner and out of sight.

"Well, hang it!" said Emily Lime, "that was a jolly old waste of . . . gah!"

She stopped walking, and shook herself like a wet dog. When she spoke again, it was in her own voice.

"Eurgh!" she said. "How can she stand it? How can Marion stand being Marion? It's so *tiring* always being jolly. And for what? It was all just a waste of time!"

"No," said George, "we didn't open the box. But—"

"But nothing!" Emily Lime snapped. "We don't need to open the box, you idiot! We already know the jewelry can't be in it. The thief would need both keys to get into it, wouldn't they? And they only had one."

"No," said Daphne. She still felt unsteady, and her voice was unsteady, too. She leaned against a lamppost for support. "I think . . ." The thoughts in her head were whirling round, adding to her dizziness. She thought again that she might be sick and pressed a hand to her mouth.

"What? What do you think?" said Emily Lime.

Daphne breathed in the smell of White's hair oil on her hand. She staggered, leaning harder into the lamppost.

"What is it?" said George.

"Lavender," said Daphne. She closed her eyes, and for a second she was back in the dark in the corridor at St. Rita's, on the night of the break-in.

"What?" said George and Emily Lime.

Daphne opened her eyes and stood straight.

"Mr. White's hair oil smells of lavender." Her voice was strong and sure now.

"So what?" said Emily Lime.

"On the night of the break-in, when I got out of the tunnel, I smelled lavender then, too. I thought it was just from the bushes outside at the time. But it wasn't. It was White's hair oil."

"Oh!" said George.

"He robbed his own bank."

"So," said George, "the loot *can* be in box 336 because White would be able to get the bank's key any time he wanted."

"We have to go to the police," said Daphne. "We have to take the key to them now, don't we?"

"Oh heck!" said George. Emily Lime and Daphne looked round at him. His hands were fumbling in his pockets and his face looked panicked. "We can't."

"Why not?" said Daphne.

"I've lost it!" said George, in a forlorn voice. "I had it in my pocket, but then I took my hanky out to wipe his bloomin' hair oil off my hand. It must have dropped out then."

He stared at them with a small, frightened expression.

"I'll have to go back in."

TWENTY-EIGHT

H e's in," said Daphne, peering in through the bank's window as George, with his blazer collar turned up in a futile effort to conceal his identity, ambled across the floor. A few of the customers gave him funny looks as he passed, though whether this was due to his appearance or his odor was unclear. "He's not exactly inconspicuous, is he?"

"No," said Emily Lime.

George was over by the door now, acting as if he wasn't desperately looking for something on the floor. He sauntered back and forth in as nonchalant a manner as he could manage, occasionally taking a casual glance at the carpet.

"Come on, George!" whispered Daphne to herself, then glanced over at Emily Lime, the tip of her nose against the windowpane, her eyes steady and intense, her lips twitching. It looked, Daphne thought, almost as if she cared.

"Hurry up, idiot!" muttered Emily Lime.

As if he had heard her, George began to pace more frantically. No longer trying to disguise his staring at the floor, he looped and circled, his head swiveling wildly. Daphne noticed someone in one of the lines nudge his neighbor and point.

As he continued to pace, George trod on a scrap of paper that attached itself to the sole of his shoe and flapped about with each step. He stopped and tried to shake it off. He stood on one leg, waggling the other foot in the air; then, when this proved unsuccessful, he tried to pick the scrap from his shoe by hand. But as he reached for his raised foot, he started to topple over. He hopped forward in an effort to stay upright but landed off balance, so he hopped again, out of Daphne's line of sight. A moment later, he came back into view, hopping back the other way, still reaching for the paper scrap, and now even more out of control.

He hopped and flapped and turned and looped, drawing more and more attention from the bored customers in the lines.

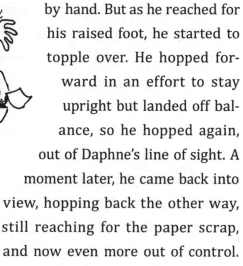

Daphne, watching from between her fingers, whimpered.

George finally plucked the scrap of paper from his shoe, grinned in triumph, and fell flat on his face. A ripple of applause drifted over from the lines.

"Oh, for heaven's sake!" growled Emily Lime.

George raised himself onto his hands and knees, then froze, his eyes fixed on the floor ahead of him. He scuttled forward, still on his knees, to a spot just in front of the back-room door.

"What is he playing at now?" hissed Daphne.

George grabbed at something on the floor. Daphne caught a glimpse of a metallic glint before George's hand closed into a tight fist.

"He's got it!" said Daphne. "He's got the key!"

"Yes," said Emily Lime. "But look!"

George, still on all fours, whipped his head up at the sound of the door opening. Mr. White, striding out purposefully with his eyes on the customers, walked straight into him. White crashed spectacularly to the floor, and the crowd went wild. George and White clambered to their feet, casting dazed glances at each other. Then White froze, his eyes locked on George's hand.

"He's seen the key!" Daphne gasped. "Get out, George! Get out, get out, get out!"

White straightened, tense and determined. George was transfixed.

Then Canning appeared in the doorway. White glanced up to wave him away, and George, as if released from a spell, ran.

White gave chase, and the two of them disappeared from view.

"Hurry, George," whispered Daphne, craning her neck in an effort to see better.

"Can you see him?" she said to Emily Lime, then realized she wasn't there. A hurried glance one way showed her Emily Lime running away from her; a look the other way showed George turning the corner from the bank's front door and sprinting desperately toward her.

"And hurry, Daphne!" whispered Daphne, and set off, racing after the receding figure of Emily Lime.

TWENTY-NINE

I s he . . . following us?" said George, who, miraculously, had caught up with Daphne as they fled away from the bank.

"I can't see him," said Daphne. She glanced back over her shoulder. "If we're lucky he didn't see which way we went. But—hey! Watch out!"

She yanked George to one side just in time to avoid being run down by a butcher's bicycle with a wide, shallow basket on the front hurtling across the sidewalk. Staring after it, she recognized the boy in a flat cap riding it.

"Lunatic!" she yelled after him as she and George set off running again.

"Clown!" the boy yelled back.

They drew up alongside Emily Lime, who had eased her pace a little.

"Heading for the station?" said Daphne.

"Yes."

"Railway . . . or police?" wheezed George.

"Railway," said Emily Lime.

"But he'll . . . probably guess that—"

"We can just make the next train to Pelham."

Emily Lime glanced behind her. Daphne did likewise. There was still no sign of White.

"But he won't make it," said Daphne. "And his car's broken down."

"Yes. We'll gain some breathing space."

"Breathing," said George. "That would . . . be nice."

Daphne looked over at him. "Are you all right, George?"

"Fine," said George, but his pained expression suggested otherwise.

"Come on!" grumbled Emily Lime. "You have to keep up!"

George gave a despairing grunt. They were heading out of town now, off toward the station on a road that sloped gently up, and the extra effort was taking its toll.

"Come on, George," said Daphne. "Just keep going a little . . . longer. You can . . . get your breath back on the train." She looked over at his red face, puffing and blowing.

"You have to go faster!" said Emily Lime. She grabbed George's arm and pulled him along with her, his legs scampering to keep up but starting to buckle beneath him.

"It's no good dragging him," protested Daphne. She looked back to see if White was anywhere in sight, and was relieved to find no sign of him. Then another familiar figure caught her eye. She peeled away from Emily Lime and George and ran toward it.

"You go on," she shouted to Emily Lime. "I'll get him there on time."

"I don't see—"

"Just go!" Daphne surprised herself with the certainty and determination in her voice.

When she came back a moment later, Emily Lime had disappeared, but George had ground to a halt and was wobbling alarmingly. Daphne sprinted toward him.

"Hang on, George. I'm coming."

George gave a faint gurgle. Then his eyelids fluttered, his legs crumpled, and he started to topple. Luckily, Daphne pushed the bicycle in his way just in time. George slumped against the wide shallow basket attached to the front of the handlebars, and sniffed.

"Sausages?" he mumbled.

"That's right," said Daphne, bracing herself to keep the bike upright. "Now, get on quick, before that wretched boy notices it's gone."

George slurred something undecipherable, but managed to crawl awkwardly up into the basket. He lay there, one arm dangling out of one side, one leg out of the other, his head lolling.

"Oi!"

Daphne turned her head to see the butcher's boy emerging from the doorway of a nearby house, then tripping over the deliveries that Daphne had unloaded onto the doorstep and falling flat on his face on the lawn.

"Just borrowing it," Daphne called over her shoulder. "Got a train to catch."

She shoved off and stood on one pedal, forcing the bicycle reluctantly into motion, bumping down from the sidewalk onto the road.

"We'll leave it outside the station for you." Another couple of turns of the pedals, and they wobbled over the crest of the hill. Daphne glanced back to check if the boy was chasing them, and saw him instead wrestling with a pack of dogs that had caught the scent of the meat. She would have smiled if she hadn't spotted White beyond him.

"He's after us!" she yelled, leaning forward and working the pedals hard.

It got easier now. The bike's wobbling eased, and they picked up a little speed, closing the gap on Emily Lime ahead of them.

"Here's our train," Emily Lime shouted back, and raised a finger to indicate a plume of smoke advancing toward the station at the bottom of the hill.

"It's going to be close!" Daphne leaned forward over the handlebars and worked the pedals harder. "Hang on tight, George!" They drew alongside Emily Lime, running steadily, then gravity lent a hand and they picked up speed and passed her.

Soon the pedals offered no more resistance, and Daphne stopped pedaling. The wind stung tears into her eyes; George's tie flailed around, whipping into her face. And still they went faster, and faster. It was exhilarating. And then it was terrifying. Daphne pulled gently at the brakes. Nothing happened, so she jammed them hard. There was a terrible screeching noise, and the bike continued to accelerate.

"Oooooooooooh!" said George.

The bottom of the hill sped toward them. There was a sharp turn to the right there, and there was no way

Daphne could make it. She wrenched the handlebars left and steered onto the verge, hoping the grass would slow them. It did, but the bicycle juddered alarmingly on the uneven ground, and now Daphne lost all control. They veered right, then left, then up against the  hedge, half in it, plowing along, leaves and twigs clawing at them. George threw his arms over his head. Daphne's senses were a chaos of noise and confusion: dark, light, noise, shaking, wind, leaves, air, light, *ow!*, dark, *ow!*, dark . . . but slowing . . . *ow!* Oh!

Only yards from the corner now. Daphne heaved the handlebars to the right, and they drew clear of the hedge and veered back toward the road. The front wheel hit a sharp dip in the ground and came to a dead stop, the back wheel leapt up, and George and Daphne were catapulted through the air to land in a heap on the grass.

They were just rising groggily to their feet as Emily Lime, still running at the same steady pace, came alongside.

"Come on! The train's here."

They scrambled after her. Daphne threw a look behind them as they reached the corner and saw White's tall, thin figure at the top of the hill, running their way. Then they were at the station entrance and straight through to the platform, where Emily Lime was already climbing into a carriage. George followed, shaking off exhaustion to step up and in. Daphne was three paces from the door—two—and then she stumbled and fell.

"Come on!" yelled George.

She scrambled to her feet and reached her arms out as she staggered forward. She took one unsteady step, another, and then grabbed at George's outstretched hand, hauling herself up and into the waiting carriage. Emily Lime slammed the door behind her, and they all fell, relieved, into their seats.

But the train stayed exactly where it was.

THIRTY

"Why aren't we moving?"

Emily Lime stood, went to the door of the compartment, and pushed down the window.

"This is the 11:23. It should depart at 11:23. It must be 11:23 and a half by now. Why aren't we moving?"

She poked her head out the window, looked along the platform in both directions, then turned back to George and Daphne.

"There are no fallen trees on the line, no earthquake or other natural disaster is occurring—we saw the train arriving, so there's no mechanical problem." Her voice was growing shrill. "I timed our arrival perfectly. The train arrives, we get on, the train departs, the dangerous criminal chasing after us is left behind at the station." She screwed her face up into a ball of frustration. "It is a beautiful plan, and I have executed my part in it perfectly. Why can't the rest of the world cooperate? WHY AREN'T WE MOVING?" she yelled.

A porter poked his head in through the open window.

"Pardon me, miss, I couldn't help . . ." He adjusted his spectacles and observed Daphne closely, thought for a moment, then smiled. "Oh, hello again, miss."

"Hello," said Daphne.

". . . couldn't help overhearing. We've just got a slight delay while the conductor gets his thermos refilled. He won't be two ticks."

"What?" Emily Lime was incensed. "What sort of a way is that to run a railway?"

"Ooh, well now, miss, old Wilf's got to have his tea, or who knows what might happen. And you'll make up the time before you get to Pelham, don't you worry."

"That's not the point! The train ought to have left the station by now!"

"Well now," the porter chuckled, "that's a point of view, I suppose, but really, where's the harm, eh? And

look, it's done this fella a favor. He'd have missed this 'un if it'd set off on time." He indicated the door to the ticket office from which the figure of Mr. White was just emerging. "So you see, it's all for the best. Oh, and here's Wilf now, too. You'll be on your way in . . ." He stared into the now-empty compartment. "Well, that is just rude."

"Here's the plan," said Daphne, crouched by the door at the far end of the carriage and peeping out the window to observe White's progress. "He's going to get on the train down there. When he's halfway along the corridor, I'll open the door and we'll jump back out and make a run for it."

"Not more running!" whimpered George. "And won't the train have set off by then?"

"Hopefully, yes," said Daphne. "With a bit of luck, it'll still be going quite slowly when we get off, but it will be too fast for him by the time he gets to the door."

"'With a bit of luck'?" said Emily Lime. "It's not much of a plan, is it?"

"Well, I'm happy to hear if you have a better one," said Daphne. "Otherwise it's all we've—"

The door opened at the far end of the carriage, and the children, as one, gasped and turned their heads to see the squat figure of Wilf the conductor climb aboard, humming happily to himself and carrying a large thermos under his arm. Seeing the trio of children, he tugged at the peak of his cap in their direction.

"Nnn . . . Hello there . . . mmm . . . miss. A pleasure to . . . nnn . . . see you again."

He advanced two steps toward them, and then White leapt aboard behind him. He stared at the children, his glowering face clearly visible above the conductor's friendly countenance.

"Excuse me," said White, brushing his hair from his face as he loomed up behind the conductor.

Outside, the porter blew his whistle and the engine began to puff and blow into life. The train lurched into slow motion, and Daphne lowered the window and leaned out and grabbed hold of the door handle.

"Get ready," she whispered.

"Oh heck!" said George.

White was right behind the conductor now.

"I say," said White. "I said, excuse me."

The conductor stopped his slow waddle toward the children and, in his own sweet time, turned to face White.

"Mmm . . . I'm sorry . . . nnn . . . sir? Can I . . . mmm . . . help you?"

"Yes!" White glared down at him. "You can get out of my way."

"Nnn . . . Certainly . . . nnn . . . sir, of . . . errrr . . . course." He didn't move an inch. "May I . . . mmm . . . see your ticket, please . . . nnn . . . sir?"

The train lurched. White swayed unsteadily backward, then forward, half stumbling, struggling to keep his balance, as the train clanked and steamed into motion.

"Can't it wait a moment?" White stared over the ticket collector's head. "I need to . . . speak to these children."

"Of course, sir. Of . . . mmm . . . course." The conductor's voice was calm and friendly. "If I could just see your ticket?"

"In a moment, I said!" snarled White, still without lowering his gaze to look at the conductor.

"I'm really so sorry, sir, but I . . . mmm . . . must just ask to see your ticket, if it's not . . . aaah . . . too much trouble."

Daphne glanced out the window, back at White, out the window again, watching the platform slipping by at a fast walking pace now. Her hand tensed on the handle.

"Well, it *is*, little man!" yelled White, at last looking down at the obstacle before him. "It *is* too much trouble! So just get out of my way, you silly little—"

White raised a hand to swat the conductor out of his way with a shove to the shoulder, but it never got that far. With remarkable speed, and while the rest of him remained absolutely still, the little man's hand shot up and took hold of White's wrist. The thermos, released from his armpit, fell to the floor.

"So sorry, sir," mumbled

the conductor in an untroubled buzz. "But I really must . . ." He looked down and saw the puddle of tea forming at his feet from the broken thermos.

"Oh! Now that is . . . mmm . . . really very regrettable." With only the tiniest movement of his hand, he turned Mr. White about-face and wrenched his arm up behind his back, making him yelp with pain. "Most regrettable indeed. If I could just take this opportunity to apologize to you for the . . . mmm . . . unfortunate nature of this exchange today."

He tweaked White's arm up just a fraction more, provoking another, louder yell. "We do endeavor to ensure the . . . mmm . . . highest degree of comfort to our passengers in normal circumstances. I really can't apologize enough."

He led White the few paces back to the door at the far end of the carriage.

"Let go of me!" screamed White.

In a blur of motion, the conductor pushed down the window with his free hand, reached out to turn the handle, and pushed the door open. Then he threw Mr. White out of the train.

"Certainly, sir," he said, and closed the door, and turned to face the children.

"I do . . . mmm . . . apologize for the commotion," he said, glancing down at the leaking thermos as he made his way toward them. "Most regrettable."

The children gaped at him. Daphne let go of the door handle and closed the window.

"Um, if I could just trouble you for your . . . mmm . . . tickets, ladies? Sir?"

"Yes!" they all said at once.

THIRTY-ONE

D o you think he's dead?" said Daphne.

George, in the opposite seat, stared out the carriage window, considering his reply. "Oh, no," he said. "Not at all."

"Not *at all* dead?" said Emily Lime.

"Not even a little bit. You heard what the guard said: He'll be fine. And he should know, he's probably pushed dozens of people off moving trains. He's a professional. And we weren't going *that* fast. *And* I think he landed on grass." George gave his chin a thoughtful scratch. "Quite a steep bank of grass that he rolled down, into gorse bushes, admittedly, and then with a pretty rocky-looking stream at the bottom—but nothing fatal. Probably."

Daphne was not entirely reassured. "But if he's not dead, then do we really want to go back to St. Rita's, where he'll know to look for us?"

"Well," said Emily Lime, "even if he's uninjured, and decides to come after us, he has no car, and the next train isn't for nearly two hours. So we'll have some time once we're back at school. In the meantime, get some sleep."

"Sleep?" said Daphne. "How can you even—"

George, his face pressed against the window, cut her short with a loud snore that resonated against the glass. Daphne was amazed. But then shortly after that, she was asleep, too.

They settled on a plan of action during the bicycle ride back to the school. They would sneak quietly in and make their way straight to Miss Bagley's office. Mrs. McKay obviously couldn't be trusted, but they had faith in Miss Bagley.

They went in the back way.

"Oh!" said George as their footsteps echoed through the still quiet of the corridor.

"What do you mean, 'oh'?" said Daphne. Then she saw. She and George came to a halt at a point where they had a clear view into four different classrooms.

"This is no time to dawdle," said Emily Lime. "We need to—"

She looked into each of the classrooms in turn.

"Oh!" she said. "Where is everyone?"

Each of the rooms was empty. And as they moved along the corridor, all the others were, too.

"This is spooky," said George, with a shiver.

"Oh!" Daphne put her hand to her mouth. "The lacrosse match!"

"Oh!" said George. "The big game against St. Walter's. The whole school was going to cheer our team on. The buses were leaving after first break."

"And you remember this only now?" said Emily Lime through gritted teeth.

"I've had a lot on my mind! But maybe, mmm ... Miss Bagley won't have gone, and she'll know what to do and ... and ... everything will be all right?"

As it happened, they had just arrived outside Miss Bagley's door. George knocked on it, and kept knocking long after the truth was clear. Then he tried the handle, but of course, the door was locked.

Then—because what else would they do?—they made their way to the library.

"So, what are our options?" said Daphne, pacing amidst the study tables.

"Well, if we go to the police," said George, "then there's the truanting to consider, and the bike theft—"

"And the bank manager thrown from a moving train," said Emily Lime.

"But *we* didn't do that!" said Daphne.

"No," said George. "But the police might think we did. One minute White's chasing me out of his bank, the next thing he's thrown from the train I'm on. It does look a bit iffy."

Emily Lime tapped a thoughtful finger against her chin. "Well, it looks iffy *for you* . . ."

"Hey!"

"But surely if we lead them to the stolen jewelry, then none of the rest of it will matter?" said Daphne.

"Maybe," said George. "If it really is in there. And if they don't just lock us up straightaway."

"But if we *don't* go to the police, then what do we do?" said Daphne. "Send the key to the assistant manager and let him sort it out?"

"And let him get the reward money?" said Emily Lime.

"Or just nab the loot himself," said George. "For all we know he's just as crooked as White."

"But if we don't take the key to the police, and we don't send it to the bank," said Daphne, "then what do we do with it?"

"Well . . ." The voice, from over by the door, was slick and cold and confident. "You could just give it back to me."

They didn't need to turn to look to know who was there, but they all did. There he was: tall, thin Mr. White, his slicked-back hair not so slicked back now, and his smart gray suit muddied and torn, but otherwise in remarkably good health.

"Oh heck!" said George.

THIRTY-TWO

How are you *here*?" said Daphne, backing away from the steps. "I thought your car was broken."

White smiled. "It is. But luckily the one I stole runs perfectly. Nevertheless, I've had a rather . . . trying day so far. So, let's keep things simple, shall we? There's no way out for you." White descended the staircase with slow menace and only a slight limp. "So why not just give me the key and no one need be hurt."

"We could try to . . . fight him, I suppose," whispered Daphne as she came alongside Emily Lime and George. "I mean, there are three of us and there's only one of him."

"Yes," said George. They continued slowly backward together. "But we're three *librarians*. We could beat him in a quiz, I should think, but fighting? Not so much."

White was at the bottom of the steps now.

"Come now, you don't want to do this the hard way."

"I have read some books about the martial arts," whispered Emily Lime. "Karate, jujitsu, aikido . . ."

"And I read a book about William Tell once," hissed George, "but you wouldn't want me to shoot an apple off your head, would you?"

George was the first to bump into the bookcase. Then Emily Lime and Daphne bumped into him. They were trapped, in the corner where philosophy met sports.

"We should have split up," said George.

"You should have thought of that earlier," said Daphne.

"Give me the key," said White, his voice steady and chilling. He didn't need to shout—he was close now, towering over them. There was a cut on his forehead that had bled for a while but then dried, and the swelling around the cut had half closed one eye. Smears of blood painted his face. His cut lip had swollen, exaggerating the sneer of his mouth. A lock of his oil-slicked

hair curled down across his face, tangled and caked in more blood. He looked ragged, and desperate, and dangerous.

"The key," he said again, still softly, and held out a hand ready to accept it.

A long forever came and went.

"All right," said George. "You can have your bloomin' key."

"George!" said Daphne, shocked.

"Well, what else am I going to do? He's going to get it anyway, in the long run. At least this way nobody gets hurt."

"Very sensible," said White, with a cold smile.

"All right. Well, hang on, then." George began to root around in his blazer pocket, and Daphne and Emily Lime stepped aside a little to give him room. First he extracted his disgusting handkerchief. "Bear with me. It's in here somewhere." He placed the disgusting rag on the shelf behind him, clumsily, almost slamming it down. Then he produced a stub of pencil and thumped that down, too. Then a boiled sweet. *Thump!* A protractor. *Thump!* Then he brought out the small, ratty paper bag, wincing as he raised it too close to his nose.

Daphne noticed at once a faint but horrible smell, and a quiet thump somewhere above her head.

"Oh, sorry, wrong pocket!" said George, slightly more loudly than was natural.

"The key!" White snarled, leaning in so that his face was only inches from George's. "Now!"

"Yes, sorry," squeaked George, rummaging in his other pocket. "Ah! Here it is!"

He held up the key, close to White's face. White grabbed at it, his eyes bulging greedily, but George snatched it away. White's face curdled into a snarl as his gaze followed the key. Then George whacked his head with the paper bag from the other side. Daphne heard a noise above her, saw the look of rage on White's face, smelled the most awful stink, and then George's arm swung into her and pushed her hard, back into the shelves. She cried out, heard Emily Lime squawk as George pushed her back, too, and all three of them slammed into the bookcase, toppling it, and fell back with it, limbs flailing.

Daphne fell with impossible slowness, observing with odd detachment the events that followed. There must have been a lot of noise, but it all seemed muffled and distant. White's face was drifting off, up and away from her, his expression shifting and re-forming, moving from fury, to surprise, to alarm. His head tilted back and Daphne, still falling, looked up, too. Two books hung in the air above her, their covers spread like wings. And past them, Daphne could see, falling, flying, leaping from the top of the bookcase, a dark blurred shape. And from the dark shape came a terrible noise,

cutting through the dull percussion of bookshelves, books, and children thumping to the floor.

"*MMRAAAOOOOOWWW!*"

The Beast hit him full in the face, claws first and screaming.

Time started up again at a normal pace, as if shocked back into life by the horrible noise of White's screams. Daphne scrabbled to her feet. George was beside her. Emily Lime was already running for the door.

Daphne followed, and she and Emily Lime were at the foot of the stairs in a moment. Behind them, the Beast's unearthly screeching, and White's cries, came to an abrupt halt. There was a loud thump, then a more distant crash, then quiet. Daphne turned on the first step and saw George crumpled on the floor, with one leg stretched out behind him, White's hand clasped around his ankle. The Beast lay dazed across the room at the foot of religion.

George kicked his foot free and crawled toward the steps, then stood, gave a sharp cry of pain, and dropped back to his knees, clutching his ankle. He flipped himself round to face White, bleeding and scarred, pacing toward him.

George thrust his arm into the air, unclenched his fist, and sent the key sailing in a high arc, spinning through the air, straight into Daphne's outstretched hands. Amazed, she closed her fingers tight around it. She shot a pleading glance at George, willing him to get away, but he was still flat on the floor. He twisted his head to look at her and gave her a narrow smile.

"Well, bugger off, then!" he said.

Behind her, Daphne heard the squeak of the door as Emily Lime went out. Before her, the jagged, raging figure of Mr. White surged toward her.

Daphne ran.

THIRTY-THREE

Y ou know, I never realized," said Daphne, running beside Emily Lime, "that being a librarian involved . . . quite so much exercise." She tried to make her voice sound more lighthearted than she felt, then felt guilty when she succeeded. "At least he came straight after us and . . . left George alone. I was worried—"

"Yes," said Emily Lime, staring straight ahead.

"Where are we going?" said Daphne.

"West staircase."

White, despite his limp, was faster than the girls, and drew closer along each section of straight corridor,

but the girls, knowing the way, pulled away a little at each corner. They still had a decent lead as they reached the staircase.

Daphne had been past it a few times and glanced at it with passing interest since the night of the midnight feast, but she had not, before now, examined it closely for signs of life-threatening danger. Now she did, and saw plenty. Some steps had rotted away almost completely, others listed to one side or the other, and the whole structure seemed unbalanced and askew.

"Just how dangerous—?"

"Very," said Emily Lime. "Pay attention. Follow me exactly." She started her way up the steps, bounding in

hopscotch-like fashion from one foot to the other, skipping over some steps, taking care only to tread on the
edges of others. Daphne followed, concentrating hard
and trying to ignore the way the staircase swayed
beneath them.

White cried out behind them as his foot crashed
through a step. Daphne looked back to see him heaving
it back out of the splintered wood and then climbing
again, but carefully now. Slowly. The girls could be out of
sight before he was even halfway up at this rate. But
when Daphne turned to face forward again she realized
she had missed Emily Lime's route up the next few steps.

"Oh, um . . . which—?"

"Keep up!" said Emily Lime, not
slowing.

Daphne took a firm hold of
the banister and raised a foot
onto the next step, pushed
gently down on it.
When she felt sure
it wouldn't col-
lapse, she stepped
up. She repeated
the process with the

next step, then the next. The step after that was almost entirely missing, so she skipped straight to the next.

Emily Lime was up on the landing now. She called down to Daphne.

"What's keeping you? You have to . . . Stop!"

Daphne's foot froze in midair.

"Middle of that one. Good. Now left. Left again . . ."

Daphne did as she was told.

"Next two are good, then right foot. Now quickly over the next three . . ."

Daphne, shaking a little from concentrating so hard, could hear White below her, still some distance behind but not as far as she would like. Only a few more steps to go.

". . . and right, and then the last few are fine . . ."

Daphne sprinted up.

". . . except the last . . ."

With a crunch, the final stair gave way beneath her foot. Daphne pitched forward, flat on her face onto the landing.

". . . one," said Emily Lime.

Daphne leapt to her feet. She wasn't hurt, just a little winded. She took in Mr. White's position, still some ways away.

"All right?" said Emily Lime.

"Yes. Thanks." Daphne felt a little light-headed with relief. "Now what?"

Emily Lime was already starting off along the landing.

"Over to the east wing, down the staircase, and over to Thanet's cottage. We can telephone the police from there."

"After we've got George from the library?" Daphne started after Emily Lime but found she was still a touch dizzy. She leaned against the banister to steady herself.

"Yes, I suppose . . ." Emily Lime cast a look back at Daphne. "No! Don't—"

There was a cracking and a crunching and a splintering sound. The worm-eaten banister gave way, and Daphne pitched backward into nothingness.

THIRTY-FOUR

Why did you have to do that?"

Daphne didn't answer. She was too busy wondering about the quality of fabric used for St. Rita's uniforms. This was not something that Daphne would usually consider, but now that she was hanging from her pinafore, snagged on the sharp end of a broken banister post, high above a stone floor, it suddenly seemed important. She dangled, upside down, scared she might fall, scared that if she did not, then she would soon be at White's mercy, and, absurdly, wondering if her knickers were showing.

"Hang on," said Emily Lime.

"To what?" said Daphne.

"No, I mean 'wait.'"

"Well, I'm not going anywhere, am I?"

Emily Lime hooked an arm around a solid bit of banister post and reached out for Daphne's ankle with the other hand.

"Hold still, for heaven's sake!"

"I'm trying!"

Emily Lime grabbed Daphne's ankle and hauled her in against the side of the landing. Daphne twisted, reached up a hand, and caught hold of the landing edge. They both pulled, and propelled Daphne back up onto the landing. She scrambled away from the edge, breathing hard, her heart beating like the clappers.

Daphne stood, her mind racing, thrilled into action by the scare. She shot a look to Mr. White, nearing the top of the staircase, then set off at a trot.

"Come on. I've got an idea."

They raced side by side past the sixth years' rooms. Behind them, Mr. White roared something that Daphne couldn't make out.

"I need to slow down," said Daphne.

"Slow down?"

"I need him close behind me . . . in the fourth-year dorm. You get the door."

"Oh," said Emily Lime. "I see. You really did have an idea."

Daphne slowed her pace a fraction, and listened to the thundering rhythm of White's footsteps as he drew closer. By the time Emily Lime reached the door, Daphne could hear his breathing. Emily Lime ducked into the dorm. Daphne snatched a look behind her as she followed, saw the roiling fury in White's face, felt his hand brush her hair. Then she was in. An extra burst of speed caught her up to Emily Lime's side, and they bolted down the aisle between the beds.

A desperate mantra ran in Daphne's head.

Don't let him see! Don't let him see!

Her lungs were bursting; she couldn't keep this up. Just three more paces.

Don't let him see!

Two more paces, one . . .

Emily Lime and Daphne leapt.

White saw the hole in the floor, but too late. He stepped onto thin air, began to fall. But as his legs dropped, momentum carried his body forward, and his chest hit the far edge. He cried out in shock and pain, and his arms flailed.

His hand found the leg of one of the beds and caught hold. His body still fell, but he held on tight. The bed scraped across the floor toward the hole. His free hand caught hold of the edge of the hole, the bed came to a halt, and he hung there, his legs dangling and kicking in space.

Then, with a grunt, he began to haul himself back up.

Emily Lime and Daphne watched from the far end of the room.

"Oh fiddlesticks!" said Daphne.

"We need to get out!" said Emily Lime. She nodded toward the beds along the far wall.

Daphne leapt onto the nearest one, then from that onto the next. She heard the creak of bedsprings behind her and knew that Emily Lime was following close behind. She leapt again.

"Will you just STOP!" yelled White. He scrambled back out of the hole and rolled himself clear just as Daphne passed, then grabbed on to the nearest bed frame and pulled himself to his feet. Emily Lime landed on the bed just as White rose up from beneath it. He dived at her, his long arms closing on thin air as she trampolined away. White crashed onto the bed, rolled off, and landed, crouched and poised, on the floorboards.

He looked to the doorway. Daphne was nearly out, and Emily Lime had reached the bed opposite. One last leap and she would be out the door. Her foot caught in a tangle of bedclothes. She belly-flopped onto the floor with a groan.

Daphne looked on in alarm from the doorway as White loomed over Emily Lime.

"Now, give me the damned key!" he roared.

Daphne looked him in the eye. Trembling, she held

up the key, drawing his gaze and his fury away from Emily Lime, who scrambled under the nearest bed.

"This?" said Daphne, waving the key in the air, then fixed him with a determined stare. "Come and get it!" She turned around and ran off. Daphne was relieved to hear Mr. White's footsteps behind her and to know that he had left Emily Lime alone. But she knew she couldn't keep running for long. She was no athlete, and she was tiring. White would catch her soon.

He was so close behind her as she approached the top of the staircase that she paid no attention to the odd thumping noise approaching from the opposite direction. Turning to head down the stairs she almost tripped over George as he hopped up the staircase in a crouched pose, hands down to steady himself. He looked up, alarmed, then relieved, and watched as Daphne dashed past him down the stairs. Then, hearing White's approach, he launched himself up the final step and grabbed at White's legs. White crashed to the floor.

George crawled free and threw a look down at Daphne.

"Hurry!" he yelled.

I'd love to! thought Daphne. But she was flagging. She couldn't outrun White any longer; she was too exhausted.

Oh, but . . .

Daphne remembered the other girls descending the staircase for the assembly. If she couldn't run . . .

She stopped, threw a leg over the banister, lay against it, and let herself go. She slid backward—fast, unsteady, and terrified.

The end came quicker than expected. The banister ran out beneath her and Daphne flew off the end. She tumbled backward, rolled, then stood. She looked up at George, shouted up to him: "Check on Emily! Fourth-year dorm!"

Behind George's shoulder, she saw White rise into view, his face full of fury.

"George! Look out!"

George turned, saw White, and threw himself out of the way, kicking out with his good leg at White's shin, just as he reached the top step. White overbalanced and threw one foot ahead of him as he began to fall. He landed two steps down, still off balance, toppled again, continued on down three or four steps at a time in rapid, uncontrolled descent, until finally, two steps from the bottom, he tripped, pitched forward, and crashed to the floor.

Daphne, lumbering away a few paces down the corridor, looked back at him, crumpled at the foot of the stairs.

Stay down! Stay down! Stay down! she thought. But White unfolded himself and rose to his feet. Daphne wanted to run but could barely manage even the thought of it now. She was too tired to run, or to think. All she could do was plod away, hoping that somehow she could escape. She saw that White was limping more now, but it wasn't enough. She was shattered. There was no hope. There was nothing she could—

Oh!

It was the slimmest chance, but it was all she had.

She had to find the right room, needed to work out where it would be. She had to remember how far along it was from the fourth-year dorm to the top of the staircase, then think about the curve of the staircase, and how far she had come along this corridor. Was it the next door on the right she needed? Or the one after?

Think, Daphne! Think!

Could she even make it to the second? White was so close now. Maybe . . .

No! She was sure it was the second door.

She begged her legs for one last effort, matched White's pace, kept ahead just long enough . . .

Don't be locked! Don't be locked!

She was at the door. She wrenched the handle round, pushed . . .

Oh, thank you, thank you, thank you!

Through, stumbling in. A quick glance upward confirmed it was the right place. Then Daphne collapsed to the floor, her lungs on fire, gasping for air.

White stood in the doorway, looked down at poor, broken Daphne Blakeway, and smiled.

"Enough," he said, and closed the door behind him.

THIRTY-FIVE

Daphne rolled over onto her back and propped herself up on her elbows to look up at White.

"How . . ." Her voice was dry and cracked. She swallowed and edged away from him, back down the clear central aisle between the rows of desks. "How do you think you can get away with this now?"

"It won't be easy," White said. He stepped toward her.

She shuffled back some more.

"It's all so . . . untidy now." He looked unsure for a moment, but then, with a shiver, shook off that passing uncertainty. "It was all meant to be so neat, but *you*—you and my *wife*, taking my books and donating them to this wretched school—you made it all so messy."

He held out a hand toward her, beckoning for the key. But Daphne looked past it at his face. The blood smears and the tense snarl of his lips frightened her, but what chilled her most was his eyes. He looked desperate, but resigned, too, as if he had nothing left to lose. As if he was capable of almost anything now.

Daphne edged back again. He followed.

"What did you do with her?" she said.

A flicker of confusion brought him to a stop. His lips parted just for a moment, but he said nothing. Then he clamped his mouth shut in a sneer and eyed Daphne with dangerous intent.

"What did you do with Veronica?" said Daphne. "What did you do with ... with her body?"

"What?" He stopped again, seemed confused, and straightened. "She's not dead. I wouldn't even have hurt her if she hadn't made me. But she was shouting my name out, the damn fool, worrying about that other girl outside the library. Didn't care that I was bleeding half to death from that . . . creature attacking me. And then she wouldn't give me the book, so I had to take it from her. So I hit her, that was all." There was a hint of uncertainty in his voice, perhaps even regret. But then it hardened again. "But you see, that's the sort of thing that can happen when people don't give me what I want."

He took another step toward Daphne.

"So, please . . ." He stretched out his hand, open palm turned up, trembling. "Just give me the key."

Daphne pushed herself back a few more weary inches. She stared at the ceiling, then flopped her head forward again to watch White's inevitable advance. She shut her mouth tight and her eyes blinked out tears, but she shook her head.

"Give me the key!" said White.

Another inch backward. Daphne clutched the key to her chest.

"Come . . ." she said in a cracked whisper. "Come and get it."

He stepped one last step toward her, balling his fists, his face tight.

"Enough," he said.

"Yes," said Daphne.

"Nooooo!" cried a voice above them.

White's eyes shot up, just in time to see George plummeting toward him. The heel of one of his shoes caught White full in the face. There was a loud, sharp crack, and White's body crumpled to the floor, with George in a heap on top of him.

"OW!" yelled George. Then he took a breath, rolled off White, and raised himself, wincing, onto his hands and knees.

"I hope that noise was his nose breaking and not my ankle," he said.

Daphne examined the prostrate body of Mr. White.

It was very still. Daphne pressed two fingers to his neck, feeling for a pulse.

"Oh blimey! I've not killed him, have I?" said George.

"No," said Daphne, and managed a feeble smile. "He's out cold, but I don't know for how long. Help me turn him over, will you, and we'll tie him up."

They rolled him over and used their ties to bind his hands behind his back and his legs together at the ankles. Then they sat admiring their handiwork, and George gave his ankles some exploratory prods as he tried to assess the damage.

"What exactly did you squish onto his head that smells so very bad?" said Daphne.

"Oh, that?" George smiled. "Well, I try to keep a few treats on me to distract the Beast if it's in a bad mood— which it always is. I think those were probably ancho-vies, but it's a while since I got 'em, so I can't remember for sure. Shame to waste them like that, but they did the trick."

"Yes. That was clever," said Daphne, standing. "And it was brave of you, jumping on him like that."

"Jumping on him?" said George. "I didn't bloomin' jump! Lime threw me!"

"You told me to!" said Emily Lime, peering down from the fourth-year dorm through the hole in the ceiling.

"I told you to throw *something heavy* at him!" said George.

"Well?"

"Are you all right?" said Daphne.

"Not sure," grumbled George. "Probably got *two* sprained ankles now!"

"But otherwise?"

George shrugged. "Nothing too serious, I s'pose." Then he grinned. "And I suppose we *have* just caught a dangerous criminal."

"I suppose we have," said Daphne.

"Yes, yes," called down Emily Lime. "That's right. Now, how much did you say that reward was?"

THIRTY - SIX

Of course, Mr. Thanet took a lot of convincing to telephone the police. And then the police took a lot of convincing to come out to St. Rita's. Eventually, though, Mr. Thanet was able to persuade them that either the children's story was true and they could at last solve the case of the bank robbery, or else it was a pack of lies and they could arrest the children for bicycle theft, assault, wrongful imprisonment, wasting police time . . . and anything else they could think of. Two police cars arrived outside the school within half an hour. George was taken to the hospital to have his ankles examined, and Mr. White, now conscious again, was judged fit enough to accompany Inspector Bright, Daphne, and Emily Lime back to the bank.

"You'll have to be quick," said Digby Canning, without looking up from the paperwork he was filling out. "It's very nearly closing time, and I've had a *very* trying day."

The man on the other side of the counter window responded only with a gentle cough.

"Very trying indeed. So, I'm afraid if it's anything at all complicated, then you'll just have to come back tomorrow."

He placed the completed form to one side and at last looked up.

"Well, Mr. Canning," said Inspector Bright, "I'm rather afraid that it may very well be complicated, as it happens. But I'll have to insist that we do deal with it today, sir. It is rather pressing."

Mr. Canning looked, at first, surprised to see the inspector; then puzzled when he recognized Emily Lime and Daphne standing behind him; then positively alarmed when he saw behind them the ragged figure of Mr. White, bloodied, bowed, and handcuffed, flanked by two constables.

Canning spent quite some time staring at White's face. One of the constables had made a brief effort to clean it with a moistened handkerchief before they had set off, and while he had successfully removed a lot of the blood, this only made clearer the disturbing new shape of White's nose. It was quite some time before Canning composed himself enough to speak.

"I see," he said. "What can I do for you, Inspector?"

"If it wouldn't be too much trouble, sir," said Inspector Bright, "then I would very much appreciate a visit to your vault."

Daphne said nothing as they all trooped down the stairs. She was tense and excited and scared, but she kept quiet. Emily Lime, ahead of Daphne, was silent, too, while White, behind her, just groaned occasionally. Canning, in any case, was doing enough talking for everyone.

"Absolutely ridiculous," he said. "Really, I've never heard anything so absurd. I shall be glad to help you put an end to this nonsense once and for all, Inspector, then you can deal with these young miscreants as you see fit."

"Indeed, sir," said the inspector.

Canning set to work unlocking the vault door, continuing his rant in installments between each turn of the dial.

"It's an outrage . . . The very idea of it . . . A pack of lies . . . And you have to ask yourself why they're so keen to point suspicion at someone else . . . What do *they* have to hide, Inspector? Eh?"

Canning took hold of the wheel on the door and gave it a turn, then pulled it open. He led them into the vault, located box 336, and produced a key from his pocket.

"Don't you worry, Mr. White, sir," he said. "We'll soon have this ludicrous business sorted out."

He pushed the key into the first keyhole. "And once we do, trust me, I'll make sure these wretches get what they deserve. Oh yes! I'll make sure that justice is done."

He turned the key.

Mr. White gave a quiet whimper.

Daphne raised the other key in a shaking hand.

"Shall I—?"

Inspector Bright took it from her.

"I'll take that, if you don't mind," he said.

Daphne watched transfixed as the inspector put the key into the vacant lock, turned it, and opened the door to the box.

"There," said Mr. Canning, "you see? There's . . ."

His face fell.

"Oh! Oh my goodness!"

They all gazed into box 336. Even in the dim light of the vault, it was a breathtaking sight. The gold and the silver, the glittering jewels and pearls, the many rings and necklaces and bangles and baubles all cast a magical glow onto their stricken faces. Daphne felt lightheaded, then realized that she probably just needed to start breathing again. As she did so, she looked round, taking in everyone else's reactions. Mr. Canning, Inspector Bright, and the two constables all gaped wide-eyed at the spectacle. Emily Lime gave a small nod of approval. Mr. White looked blank, and groaned.

"Well," said Inspector Bright at last. "I think, Mr. White, that you had better come along to the station with us for a little chat. We'll need to speak with you, too, in due course, Mr. Canning."

"Of—of course, Inspector," gulped Mr. Canning.

"We'll just lock this back up for now, shall we?" said the inspector, doing so without waiting for a reply. "And I'll hold on to both keys for the time being. We'll send a team back shortly to take the full details of the stolen items and take them into evidence. Will you be able to stay here in the meantime, sir?"

Mr. Canning nodded mutely, and propped a hand against the wall to steady himself.

"Mr. White," said the inspector, "I wonder if you'd be so kind as to tell me something right now, just to be going on with?"

Mr. White turned his weary, battered face to the inspector.

"What?" he said.

"If I were to assume that you felt no need to wear gloves when you committed the robbery and that these items will be generously covered in your fingerprints, would that be right, sir?"

White winced, and gave a small defeated nod.

"Well, that's very helpful of you, sir. Thank you very much indeed. Constable Gibbons, could you escort these young ladies back to St. Rita's for me? Their statements can wait, for the time being." He gave Emily Lime and Daphne a little bow of the head. "We'll be in touch shortly."

"About the reward?" said Emily Lime.

"About, miss," said the inspector in a stern voice, "your own version of events, and about why you acted quite so foolishly and recklessly for so long before bringing any of this business to our attention." Then he smiled, just a little. "And, yes, about the really very substantial reward."

Emily Lime nodded.

"Right, then," said Inspector Bright. "Constable Brierley, if you'd be so kind, let us take Mr. White to the station with all haste (but with due deference to prevailing speed limits and the strictures of the Highway Code). Thanks for your help, Mr. Canning. Good day."

"And good day to you, Inspector," muttered Mr. Canning, though from his expression it was clear that for him, actually, it had not been a good day at all.

THIRTY-SEVEN

I see they're back from the match, then." Daphne pointed out the police car window at the coach parked outside the front of St. Rita's. "Oh, mind the hole, Constable Gibbons."

The car swerved just in time round the dip in the drive.

"Thank you, miss," said Constable Gibbons. "Subsidence, is it?"

"Chemistry experiment," Daphne and Emily chorused.

As Constable Gibbons pulled up behind the coach, Mrs. McKay, looking fearsome, and Miss Bagley, looking flustered, emerged from the school at speed, stomping toward the car.

"Oh crumbs!" said Daphne as she and Emily Lime climbed out. "The welcoming committee doesn't look very welcoming." She aimed her best fake smile at the head. "Hello, Mrs. McKay. How did the lacrosse go?"

Mrs. McKay ignored her and addressed Constable Gibbons.

"Thank you so much for bringing these wayward girls back to us, officer. I do apologize for the trouble, and I assure you that we will be disciplining them both very harshly indeed for whatever—"

"Oh, they're not in any trouble, miss." Constable Gibbons took off his cap and stashed it in an armpit. "Quite the opposite, in fact. These here girls have helped solve a crime and bring a dangerous criminal to justice, and will, in due course, be receiving a substantial reward."

"Good gracious! But just the same, I'm afraid—"

"Where's George?" Miss Bagley's voice was racked with worry. "Is he all right?"

"Yes, yes," said Emily Lime.

"Well," said Daphne. "He *is* in the hospital."

"Oh lord!" said Miss Bagley.

"The clumsy oaf hurt both his ankles," said Emily Lime. "They took X-rays and they're only sprained."

"They radioed to the car on the way here to tell us." There was a tinge of excitement in Daphne's voice. "He's going to be fine."

Miss Bagley's face softened with relief. "Oh, thank goodness," she muttered.

"That's all very well," grumped Mrs. McKay. "But the pair of you will be lucky if you're not expelled. And as for your supposed heroic crime-fighting deeds: I think you will find that as they were performed during term time, any financial reward is, in fact, due to the school and not . . . Oh, what now?"

Daphne turned to see what had distracted Mrs. McKay and saw that the other police car, carrying Inspector Bright and Constable Brierley, was racing down the driveway toward them. It skidded to a halt, and the policemen emerged.

"Hello, Inspector," said Daphne.

"Agatha McKay?" There was an unnerving purpose to Inspector Bright as he strode toward the head.

Mrs. McKay clearly spotted it. Her lips twitched as if she was about to speak, but then, after one brief wordless squeak, she turned and ran.

"Look lively, Brierley," said the inspector, indicating the fleeing head with an unflustered wave of the hand. The constable sprinted off after her.

Daphne looked on bemused as Brierley chased the head past the school building and over a good stretch of field before bringing her to the ground in an undignified heap with a well-timed rugby tackle. Inspector Bright gave an approving nod and turned back to Emily Lime, Daphne, and Miss Bagley.

"Now," he said, "I daresay you might be interested in an explanation . . ."

How much? said George.

Daphne grinned and repeated the number.

"Crikey on toast! Really?"

"Yes," said Emily Lime. "Really."

They were in George's bedroom. It was a small room, tucked in amongst the staff bedrooms, and exactly as untidy as Daphne had expected. George was lying on the bed with both bandaged feet raised up on pillows. Emily Lime stood at the foot of the bed, Daphne to one side, Miss Bagley by the door.

"And we can spend all of it on the library?"

"Every penny," said Miss Bagley, grinning. "And we'll spend the insurance money on general repairs. Finally get the roof fixed and so forth."

"The insurance money?" George looked puzzled.

"Yes. You know that phrase 'helping the police with their inquiries'?" Miss Bagley stepped closer to the bed. "Well, Mr. White really did. He told Inspector Bright that Mrs. McKay had acted very suspiciously just after the library burned down. Rented a safe-deposit box at the bank. It turns out the insurance company did pay out after all. Mrs. McKay just said they didn't and stashed the cash in the deposit box."

"So she's been arrested for fraud!" Daphne made no attempt to hide the delight in her voice.

"And hopefully arson, too," said Emily Lime.

"Mrs. McKay started the fire?" George looked astonished.

"It's starting to look that way," said Daphne.

"Imagine it: deliberately burning books!" Emily Lime shuddered. "What kind of sick monster could do such a thing? They should throw away the key."

"And what about Veronica?" said George.

"Oh, I'm all right."

Everyone turned in the direction of the doorway, which now framed Marion and Veronica, both beaming.

"Ronnie!" Daphne beamed right back at her.

"A constable just dropped her off," said Marion. "Thought you might want to say hello."

Daphne grabbed her by the shoulders and took a closer look at her, noting now the bruise on her cheek. "Oh, but . . ."

"That's not so bad," said Veronica. "I'm just glad to be out. Uncle Ian had me locked in the cellar after the break-in. I thought I might be there for weeks. I know I should never have agreed to help him get his book back, but after he tried before and almost scared Mrs. Crump to death, I thought the safest thing would be to make it easy for him. So I got Hulky to swap the labels on the jars of chemicals and cause the explosion in the chemistry lesson, to make sure there'd be a window open for him, and that was meant to be the end of it."

"Oh, but then you saw I had the book," said Daphne. "So you took it and slipped away to take it to him."

"Yes." Veronica looked sheepish. "I felt bad about it, really I did. But I honestly thought it was for the best. Of course, then it turned out that it was the wrong book anyway, so that served me right!"

"Don't be daft, petal," said Miss Bagley. "We're all just glad you're safe."

"So, mmm . . . Miss Bagley," said George, "if Mrs. McKay's gone, does that mean you're in charge now?"

"For the time being, George, yes." Miss Bagley gave them all a knowing look. "Which means I may even be too busy to worry too much about any mentions of larder raids, tunnels, or chemistry explosions—for now. But for goodness' sake, *try* to behave yourselves from now on. Especially you, Daphne. You've only been here three days, and you've already turned the place upside down."

"Sorry, miss."

"Yes, well . . . you're not really, though, are you?"

"Not much, miss, no."

Miss Bagley grinned. "No. Well, good for you, flower. But don't tell anyone I said so."

"Good show!" said Marion. "Well, I'd love to stay here chitchatting, but I said I'd meet Cicely for some of that abominable grub they serve up in the dining hall. Anyone want to join me?"

"Well, um, I shan't," said George, waving at his bandaged feet.

"Ah well," said Miss Bagley, "you've no need to anyway. I've arranged room service for you." She gave George a knowing grin. "The rest of you, off we go and we'll leave this clot to his recovery." She waved a hand at the door and Marion led them out.

A short way down the corridor, they passed Cynthia Rawlinson coming the other way carrying a tray full of food and wearing an expression of deep annoyance.

"You're making Cynthia wait on George?" giggled Daphne. "I can't imagine she's very happy about that."

"Do you think?" Miss Bagley smiled innocently. "That hadn't occurred to me at all. Although, now you mention it, I don't suppose George will be best pleased about it either." Her smile broadened to a mischievous grin.

When they arrived outside the dining hall, Emily Lime turned away.

"Aren't you coming in for some supper?" said Daphne as the others went in.

"No time. Far too much to do in the library. Oh, but..."

"What?"

"... I've got your badges." Emily Lime rummaged in her pocket and then pinned to Daphne's dress a battered and scratched enamel badge with the words

Assistant Librarian on it. Then above it she pinned, at a wonky angle, a second badge, half the height of the first, with the word *Assistant* on it.

"Assistant assistant librarian," said Daphne.

"Yes," said Emily Lime.

"It's official, then?"

"Subject to the satisfactory completion of your probationary period, naturally," said Emily Lime. She shook Daphne awkwardly by the hand, then marched off without waiting for a reply.

"Naturally," said Daphne, and watched Emily Lime's figure disappear off down the corridor. "Welcome to St. Rita's, Daphne Blakeway." She looked down at her new badges and smiled. "Assistant assistant librarian."

Then she held her breath and went in to supper.

Acknowledgments

Very many thanks (in alphabetical order) to:

Mila Bartolomé Smy, Bronwen Bennie, Julia Bruce, Jasmine Denholm, Phil Earle, David Fickling, Rosie Fickling, Anthony Hinton, Simon Mason, Bella Pearson, Woodrow Phoenix, Alan (Fred) Pipes, Pam Smy, and Ness Wood, who have been variously essential, helpful, supportive, and/or extraordinarily patient during the making of this book.